THE FACELESS MOON

EXILES: VOLUME TWO

ASHLEY CAPES

For the Backers!

CONTENTS

PROLOGUE – ANYO

Anyo stared across the green meadow with its bright flowers, each appearing almost joyous beneath the afternoon sun. And yet, he was unable to take a single step into that meadow, not a single step to follow Mei or the creature, or Marhyn... not a single step away from Rinbe's home and the tomb below.

Footsteps drew near; Han, his white beard split by a smile. "Still here, then? You need to decide soon if we want to use the afternoon to make a start."

Anyo nodded. "True." He glanced at the bandage upon Han's arm. "How are you feeling now?"

Han flexed his arms, one after the other. "Better than I imagined. Whatever that thing was, it had some mighty poison, but I'm close enough to recovered now."

"Me too."

"Still think she was a sun-killer?"

"I am less certain than I once was, I admit." Anyo shrugged. "Part of me wants to follow her to offer thanks, part to discover the truth."

"But?"

"But another path lies before us now."

Hanibalo chuckled. "So you say, yet we've been ready to leave for long enough, don't you think? Katonga can only relieve himself so many more times while waiting."

Anyo smiled. "That is fair."

"Then you're really going to turn your back on this place to chase that girl?"

"For now, we're leaving," he replied. "But not to follow Mei, no. We're returning to the snake-pit some still call Omaila."

"I see. The capital is still a risk, isn't it? Your father and probably half your siblings, not to mention the citizens. And why now?"

"The cost of my hubris."

"Anyo?"

He turned back to Rinbe's home, the stone still covered in dark needles from the fir. "At the very least, it was quite foolish of me to come here."

"Oh?"

"Of course," he said with a shrug. "Convinced that no-one else had come so far before, convinced that *I* would succeed where others had failed. Even hidden as this valley was, we cannot have been the first to find Rinbe's resting place in the *many* years since he died. It was never the location, Han, but the tomb itself that stopped people from recovering Sothalic."

Han exhaled. "That might be true. If so, what does the very place we left offer?"

Anyo hesitated. *Only one choice remains – I'm not again risking everything on another foreign sorcerer like Marhyn.*

There had been someone who offered help, back in the city.

Refusing her assistance at the time was the obvious decision – or so it seemed – before leaving to prepare for his search over a year ago. Yet now, after such a clear defeat, after such bitter disappointment, it was enough to have him considering Binya after all.

Not only a suspected Takirov spy, but something worse – a corpse-singer. And the cost of her service was… unpleasant. More, an unknown. Possibly fatal, after a fashion. Yet who else could unlock the secrets of the past? "Binya."

Han folded his arms across his chest. "No, lad. We both know that is a mistake. And immoral. *And* it is exactly why we left her behind in the first place."

"I know that, certainly," he replied. "And I know now that we have few other choices."

"There is always a choice."

"You mean letting go? Giving up on the Sothalic? On my heritage? Of changing the city?"

The older man nodded.

"I cannot do that."

Han frowned. "Then who will pay Binya's price? Are you volunteering?"

"She can be convinced to accept something else."

"And if she cannot?"

"Then, yes. I will pay her price myself."

CHAPTER 1. – MEI

Swallowing cut into Mei's throat and mouth as she drove herself across the barren plain but the dryness was not eased by blood from the inside of her lip, saliva, or her tears of exhaustion.

Just how long have I been running? Is it morning or noon? And which day?

Despite the haze that had fallen across her mind, she was still able to recognise when her surroundings changed. *I'm so close.* She squinted as a glint of light caught her eye. Sparkling water! At last, the river she'd seen from the hills.

Mei stumbled across the sandy earth only to fall, rolling the final few paces and splashing into the shallows with a sob of relief.

The cool of the river spread across her skin like a balm. She simply lay still for a moment, water lapping at her chin until she turned her head to drink. It soothed her throat, and fresh tears mixed with the water now, but it was a deep, deep relief. No need to hurry back to her feet; the current was not so strong within her clear little pool, the shallows no threat – the water was life itself.

Eventually, she sat up to splash more water on her face and arms. She wiped at the thin trails of mud next. *I survived.* A blessing. All thanks to the river. She glanced along its silvery length where reeds huddled together farther on and the far bank held more greenery. Had Iggy lay within a similar pool, on the very same river? Had he even travelled west?

He has. I hope.

And hope was all she had.

Leaving the marsh after two days of trekking, becoming lost in sucking mud or deep rivulets and channels, after avoiding diseased-looking plants and surviving on little but stolen water, Mei had stumbled free of the Malkaha without any clear sense of where she was. Or where Iggy had gone. She couldn't sense her brother at all, had no idea if he'd stayed with rivers or sought towns. Mei knew nothing of the Nasaru lands, and carried no map.

Finding her way *anywhere* might still prove impossible.

Escaping Anyo and his men had been far easier.

Before fleeing Rinbe's valley, Mei had tended to her former captors, careful not to let the green murk touch her hands while cleaning Anyo. And when she had tipped the pot she used over some grass, the blades began to wilt. They didn't hiss or blacken right away... but it did not seem they would survive unscathed.

Back inside Rinbe's abandoned home, she'd collected the supplies she'd taken from the Nasaru – leaving at least some food behind – and set off with only a final glance. All three men were breathing, even if not a single one could actually move.

"You're on your own now," she had murmured as she left.

The same supplies had been enough to get her through damp nights in the swamp, shivering and slapping at gnats once more. But by the time her flight took her to an animal trail and into empty hills where tired-looking bracken clung to grey dirt, her food was gone.

Her water lasted long enough to reach the dusty plains below, and then it was just the sun fuelling her as she'd lurched through the dry grass and over the occasional hill. Enough to finally reach the nameless river and collapse within.

Despite the ache in her stomach, food could wait.

She had water now. "This is wonderful," she murmured, and her throat no longer hurt as much.

If she followed the river, sooner or later she'd find a village, town or city... but it would be full of strangers, none of whom would be likely to help let alone understand her. She would be seen as Senoja and treated with suspicion at best.

So, too, a chance existed that Anyo had recovered and followed her, was even now closing in. She had to find Iggy, and soon.

Once again, Mei let her senses expand, pushing them across and up and down the sparkling river toward greener land, hoping for a sense of his enormous power, calling out his name in her mind, but as before, there was no answer.

I'm one of the strongest in the village but it's not enough. Was there another way? Simply roaming Nasaru without any method to trace Ig was hopeless. She needed help. Someone more powerful.

She frowned. Would that mean returning home?

Hadn't Paragon Lirafi worked with Mikal to find old Uganl when the man had wandered off into the abandoned fields to the south? How had they *joined* their telepathy? It had been many years ago, the details were vague.

Mei smashed a fist into the water.

It didn't matter. *I am not going back there.*

"Denuko was right."

Seeking Iggy all by herself *was* nearly impossible. Sitting in a river with only a few possessions, no knowledge of the Nasaru language and no-one to call upon wasn't going to solve anything. Mei reached into her inner vest where the silver coin from Denuko rested – Anyo not having bothered to take the money.

There had to be a way to use it… to pay someone to help her find a sorcerer? She straightened. To pay a sorcerer directly? Anyo had done something similar with Marhyn and the guiding object, the one she'd never got a clear look at.

The solution might have been staring her in the face the whole time.

The barrier of language remained, true enough, but Mei stood and started back to the shore, water trailing, and with a new snap to her step.

I just have to keep moving now.

An old trail ran beside the river and she followed its weaving path. The water was broadening, growing deeper and darker. Scattered leaves from the few willows lining the banks flowed downstream; she travelled no woodland, but toward the west, a great green haze waited.

When the sun reached its blazing peak, mostly having dried her clothes, Mei paused to wipe sweat from her brow. She'd reached a small wood that crossed the river. Its shade would be both welcome and a slight drain upon her strength, which had only grown as the sunlight granted her body energy.

At the edge of the wood, a timber bridge spanned the water. It had been built sturdy enough for a wagon, and led to a paved road south – one that disappeared upon the plain. To the north, the same road was swallowed by the trees.

Which path would take her to a village or town? How many sorcerers could be found in any given village? She faced the stretching plains. No answers in the wilted grass or occasional stand of dark trees. What lay farther west of the Malkaha? Bigger towns and cities, probably.

But she had to keep close to the river. Crossing the bridge and heading north would at least offer a chance to see what, if anything, might wait nearby. Perhaps a forest-village? If not, turning back to get access to water and heading west once more was not going to be a problem.

Decision made, Mei set off across the bridge at a jog. Her now well-and-truly dry boots thumped against the boards but at the midway point, she faltered.

A hooded figure appeared from the trees on the far bank, stepping from behind one of the gnarled-looking trunks. They wore a dark-yellow cloak over a black tunic and carried a two-pronged spear.

Mei resumed at a walk and drew a little closer. She noted that while the hood concealed much of the figure's face, a dark beard and tanned skin was visible.

It did not seem he was a villager, or traveller native to Nasaru lands. Did he hail from farther north? From Cresideth, like Marhyn? Supposedly a strange land of red sails upon searing deserts, beautiful glittering oases and tangled jungles. As a child, the stories of Cresideth had been among her favourites.

The swift sand-boats and winged cats or giant butterflies, or the stories claiming everyone could speak to animals…

Yet the man before her seemed, aside from his striking cloak and hood, far more… ordinary. And when she reached the far side of the river, passing close by, he did not speak, nor raise his hood, but offered a smile and a nod.

Mei returned the greeting with a nod of her own and continued along the road.

She glanced back once, but the fellow was already crossing the bridge. A small sparrow swooped down to follow… or was it merely flying in the same direction? She released the grip she'd taken on her power. "Oh." *I was ready to strike…*

Deeper into the wood, her way remained clear and unmarred by much in the way of holes or ridges or other obstructions. Instead, it was half-covered in leaves with rounded edges and small nuts wearing funny little helmets.

She did not have to walk far before coming across a wooden sign with three panels. The words upon it made no sense but surely they would relate to villages or towns and cities ahead.

Perfect. She hurried forward, and buildings *did* soon appear ahead; maybe thirty or more wooden homes with thatch rooves surrounded a dirt-square with a large well. Larger than Nokema, the village was busy with people in dark smocks and boots, moving to and from the well and one even hurrying into the trees with a large saw set across his shoulder.

Mei stopped near the first home, where a woman knelt in her garden tossing weeds onto a pile. How to actually ask for help? Mei hesitated, and before she could even attempt to speak or gently approach, the woman looked up, then frowned. She spoke a few words.

Still Mei hesitated.

Now the woman rose, one hand on her hip as she waved a hand, as if to dismiss Mei.

"I'm sorry, but I need help," Mei said, the useless words slipping out.

"*Onima!*" the woman snapped.

Mei strode away, moving farther into the village – the woman's tone had been clear, if not the exact meaning.

Near the well now, Mei slowed as more and more eyes fell upon her. Frowns and glares followed. *I'm obviously not welcome here.* But no-one approached, nor spoke. They simply watched. One of those watchers was an older man whose expression was comparatively friendly. He leant against the well, carving a piece of wood with a short knife.

I'm most likely in danger, even if they don't show it.

There was a bucket at the well she could fling at someone, if needed.

Or half a dozen tools hanging from belts. She could probably whip up a cloud of dust even, to scare them instead of lashing out and striking their minds, since such an attack might not be the best first choice... And how many could she stop that way before collapsing herself? Her arms were trembling.

Mei stilled them with some effort. Lashing out first was a mistake. *I have to make them understand without violence. I just need one person to help me find a sorcerer, that's all!*

The carver flinched. "*Dormatta?*"

Mei blinked. Had he understood her thought, had she pushed it out? She spoke again, asking the same question, but the villager's look of vague comprehension and confusion faded. He paused his carving to rub at his temples.

I need to find a sorcerer, can you help me? Mei asked as she moved a little closer. This time, she sent the words from her mind toward him consciously – and the old man fell back.

She raised her hands. *Please.*

The Nasaru man glanced at his fellow villagers with wide eyes and Mei did too but everyone seemed to be getting back to their business. He looked at her then, perhaps having come to accept that no-one else could hear her voice, then pointed to a large building with many windows. A sign with the head of a bear hung above the door, unintelligible Nasaru script below.

"Gi-lo-am," he said, speaking slowly.

Gilo-am?

He nodded. "Giloam."

Is that who I need to see? In that building?

The man shook his head with a frown. But it didn't seem he'd given up, since he then snapped his fingers, before bending to one knee. There, he gestured and she knelt with him. Using the point of his knife, he drew a small circle in the dirt. Next, he slid a line with a few curves, stopping to create a larger circle.

Then he pointed to Mei, and himself, and then the small circle.

Ah, are we there? In the small circle?

He smiled as he nodded. Then he slid his finger to the larger circle. "Giloam."

And that's where I can find a sorcerer?

Once again, he nodded.

Mei smiled back at him. *Thank you.* She looked to the large building. *Will someone inside that building take me there? I have a little money only.*

The villager spread his hands, then pointed to the building... or perhaps at the man with the merchant's collar who was exiting. "Mamalo."

Is that the name of the merchant that can take me to Giloam?

He spoke a single word with another nod, a word that might have been 'yes' or 'goodbye', or anything really, but he was rubbing at his temples once again and pain glittered in his eyes.

He resumed his carving.

"Thank you!" Mei said, relief flooding her voice, then strode toward the merchant.

CHAPTER 2. – MEI

The merchant glanced over his shoulder when Mei called his name, then turned back to the work of hitching his horses to the cart. He paused to rub their necks, murmuring softly.

"Excuse me, Mamalo?"

He turned then, one eyebrow raised as he spoke, the words meaningless. His collar was similar to Denuko's, with a set of scales and Nasaru numbers. But unlike Denuko, this merchant wore no beard and the hair on his head had been shaved close. And though his face seemed kind enough, his words held traces of impatience.

But it did seem he asked a question, at least.

Mei lifted her one and only silver coin. *Can you guide me to Giloam? I must find a sorcerer there.*

The merchant's eyes widened, but he did not flinch as the villager had. Instead, he motioned for her to put the coin away with a smile. His next question was again unfamiliar, save for the word "Senoja".

Mei hesitated. *Is he asking about me? Should I lie? Does he think I'm a spy too?*

The man waited.

I can't understand you.

He shrugged and gestured to the driver's seat.

You'll take me to Giloam?

He nodded.

For money?

The merchant shook his head, as if to suggest that he expected none. And now Mei hesitated. Could he be trusted? She could break bones or stun his mind with her power, but only if she struck first, only if she knew an attack was coming. *What if he plans to be kind at first, only to turn me over to the first group of soldiers he sees? Or worse?*

Mamalo spoke again, and this time he climbed up onto the bench and took the reins. He continued speaking a moment longer, then trailed off. With a sigh, he hopped back down and rummaged around within the back of the wagon.

When he returned, the merchant held a blanket of pale blue, the pattern of a blazing sun stitched in white in the centre. *We make these at home.* She took and examined the blanket – two colours in the cross-stitching. Mei looked up at the merchant. *This looks like Inora work.*

A nod.

Are you saying… you know that I am not Senoja?

He nodded again.

But you'll keep my secret?

The merchant smiled as he answered, a single word which sounded like 'Eu' and probably meant 'yes'.

Why?

Mamalo gestured to the rest of the village and shrugged.

He was trying to tell her that she had little choice, it seemed. And he was right. A place with no name she could learn, let alone the names of those who might help. Assuming any would. *I could still take the road out of the village and keep walking myself...*

Something rumbled beneath her feet. Faint, but approaching at speed. Hooves?

Mamalo's head snapped toward the sound. He took a few steps along the road, and Mei shaded her eyes as she looked after. Steel gleamed between the trees, visible for fleeting moments only.

The merchant spun and caught her by the shoulders, speaking in a stern voice, his concern clear. He gestured to the back of the wagon, drawing her close before shoving a large crate to one side. Then, he hauled her up into the back before she could object, motioned for silence with a finger held to his lips. He pulled the canvas cover closed.

Mei blinked. Mamalo had moved *fast*.

Shock as much as anything else had kept her from lashing out, that and the worry in his voice, meaningless as the words remained. The riders concerned him – why? *It's obvious, you fool. He doesn't want you to be seen.* Which meant soldiers.

She waited in the dim wagon, lying still as possible.

The scent of cinnamon and lavender filled the space, along with something else she could not place – sharp but not overpowering. Whatever Mamalo sold didn't seem to be something so dangerous that the soldiers would be chasing him. So, were they just passing through the village? On patrol?

Or could it even be Anyo, somehow come to the village seeking her?

That doesn't seem as likely.

The hooves came to a halt, horses snorting, but raised

voices soon overtook the sound of the animals. By the coarse impatience, it seemed the soldiers were demanding answers from any and all.

Mei shifted slightly, finding a tiny opening in the canvas and peering through. She caught a glimpse of armour and the rump of a horse, its tail swishing, but nothing else. One of the villagers spoke to the soldiers, and when she finished, the horses set off once more, their hoof-beats soon fading.

A moment longer and then the covering parted, revealing a smiling Mamalo.

He extended a hand and Mei accepted his help, though it wasn't really necessary. She waited while he tied the opening down once more. Was he trustworthy? More so than she was willing to admit?

Hiding her from the soldiers was something, but he likely worried about being seen helping a possible spy.

On the other hand, he did not seem to want any money...

Mei followed him around the wagon and when he took the driver's seat, she hesitated just a moment before climbing up beside him. She had to find a sorcerer, and she had no idea where she was or where she was going. Those soldiers wouldn't be the last she would encounter either. Maybe this man could help, and if he turned out to be duplicitous, Mei wasn't defenceless.

Mamalo gave her a nod as he snapped the reins. The wagon rolled from the village, wheels crunching over dirt and gravel, then a bump as it settled onto the road – she gripped the seat as the horses moved into a trot. Overall, it was a little faster than any childhood rides she'd taken on Denuko's wagon, but soon enough she grew accustomed.

Unable to easily converse with the merchant, Mei settled for focusing on her surroundings as the now thinning woods rolled by. It was not a forest, precisely, considering the long stretches of grass, weeds and stones without trees, but when the wagon did pass through shaded stretches of road, shadows were cast by trees with gnarled trunks beneath green leaves and more of the nuts, some a paler green and others a golden brown.

So different from the Glass Forest.

But the same river she'd collapsed within not so long ago ran nearby, sometimes close enough to see, usually only audible beyond the trunks or dipping into valleys the merchant skirted. He kept to what was a main road, though travellers were infrequent – usually villagers or perhaps farmers – and all of whom paid them little heed.

And it seemed, too, that other small towns or villages were nearby. Wooden markers sat at the heads of other trails, or even fences that surrounded fields and distant homes of stone.

By the time evening cast its orange glow, Mamalo had found a campsite that seemed well-used. It boasted a wide, open space ringed by trees and a cloven hunk of stone half the size of a boulder at one end. There, a blackened fire-pit with an arch waited. Cut into the stone, there was even an alcove filled with chopped wood. Perhaps left behind by a previous traveller. A plaque rested above the alcove, but she could not read it from her seat – nor from up close, no doubt.

The merchant climbed down and began to unhitch the horses.

How can I help? Mei asked.

He paused, as if in thought.

The question was likely too vague – it shouldn't have been

a surprise that he had no ready answer. *Stupid of me.* Better to ask something where a 'yes' or a 'no' was the answer.

But Mamalo still responded with 'Eu' and led her to the rear of the wagon. There, he shifted two large barrels of water, one of which was half-empty, and lifted free a string of flasks. He spoke a few words, glancing toward the river.

She nodded in understanding and took the flasks, heading for the water's edge where she knelt and dunked them one-by-one. How long would it take to reach Giloam? What would it be like? *And once I get there, how can I explain to a sorcerer what I need?* Money was another problem. What could a single silver coin amount to?

Mei returned for the large, half-empty barrel next. That took a bit more work but once she'd filled it, she rejoined the merchant, who was cutting carrots with his belt knife. He nodded toward a small pile of steel poles – wards, just like those used by Denuko.

I remember these. She sent the words to his mind and he smiled.

Once Mei had driven them one by one into the loam, hoping they were spaced around the camp correctly, she returned and found a pot, which she filled with water and hung over the fire.

Mamalo prepared a meal of meat and vegetables, most of which she recognised from home, and they ate in silence for the most part.

Darkness had fallen and the stars glittered above when Mei finished and attended to cleaning up. She motioned for Mamalo's attention. *How long will it take to reach Giloam?* She lifted a small stick and drew the line between two circles, copying the image the villager had drawn as best she could. She pointed at the larger circle. "Giloam."

"Hmmm." Mamalo held out his hand and she gave him the stick. He drew three circles leading to Giloam and then rested the stick on the first and raised a single finger. Next, he rested his cheek upon folded hands, closing his eyes.

Sleep... one sleep to the first village or town?

He smiled and offered a single word in response, which sounded like agreement.

Next, he moved to the second circle and raised three fingers and mimed 'sleep' once more.

Three nights.

And finally, to the last circle before their destination, where he raised only one finger. Then, he returned to the middle circle and pointed to Mei, opened and closed one hand while pointing to his mouth, repeating the motion. What did he mean... he was miming speech!

I can speak to someone there? Someone who I will understand?

Mamalo shook his head.

He tried again, and this time it seemed he included a third person, while still motioning between them all with the mime that stood for speech, but Mei shook her own head, unable to follow.

He shrugged with a small smile, then led her to the rear of the wagon. There, he pulled back the canvas to reveal a bedroll nestled between his wares – a similar arrangement to how she'd travelled with Denuko.

Mamalo gestured for her to sleep.

Oh. Where will you sleep?

The merchant jerked a thumb over his shoulder and toward

the fire with a smile.

Thank you for this, Mamalo.

He nodded and returned to the fire-pit where he spread out a bedroll. Mei hopped up into the wagon and settled herself, lying back with a sigh. Her own head was aching; not from the cinnamon and lavender but the extra effort of communicating, of not quite understanding, of being unsure. It had all taken its toll. Mamalo, too, must have been weary – her telepathy had that effect on the carver from the village, at least.

Sleep still did not come swiftly.

A trace of concern remained. The merchant *could* be trusted, it seemed. He was patient and kind, and something about him was calming... he was no gaffer but he wasn't a young man either. Was there... something fatherly about Mamalo? Even so, it did not automatically make him trustworthy. *There's always a chance he's simply been playing nice for now...*

Mei listened. A faint breeze moved the canvas and somewhere a night bird sang out but there were no other sounds. She sat up, straining her hearing, but still nothing. Then a soft snoring reached her, and she lay back with a small smile.

The merchant was already asleep, and the wards were in place... she was safe enough, surely.

Mei sighed and closed her eyes.

CHAPTER 3. – THORN

Using light to travel from the marsh and back to the capital, after only a short detour to retrieve his store of jewels, made for a sharp contrast upon arrival. One moment, Thorn was hauling himself free of the marsh and its damp rot, the next descending a set of stairs within one of the quieter gardens, dust rising with each step. A curious but welcome effect of the Inora travel was for mud and other liquids to sometimes transform into dust during the 'flight'.

For those who bothered to stare at him as he left the collection of statues, they saw only a Nasaru man half-covered in dust, not King Mutolo, and certainly not Thorn.

Ahead, a family sat eating at a long table, their smiling faces reaching him even from a distance. The sight cut into him with a suddenness that gave him pause. To have turned so conclusively away from something… and so long ago… even little hooks could lay hidden for years, for decades at a time, to dig in when least expected.

He detoured the moment of joyfulness, using a row of flower beds to at least offer a warm, sweetness to his passage. The blooms had been arranged in reds, yellows and pinks, rising in small tiers that encouraged birds and insects alike to visit.

Similar rows of flowers filled the streets beyond the garden, dividing the stone thoroughfare that led, eventually, to the palace. It peered over the people, horses and carriages, the gleaming building waiting like a lure, almost unbearable beneath the noon sun.

Yet, to be honest, the palace did not seem more than the sum of its spires.

From one tower to another, its windows and famous Eternal Silks were similar enough – a forest of gold, silver and soft, sky blue – but there was little function to the place. One tower rarely connected to another. Even the base buildings with their graceful, sweeping lines were perhaps more concerned with sigils and crests upon the stone rather than wide entryways for delivery of goods or reception of dignitaries, absent even of walls to repel invaders.

That had been left to the city's own perimeter.

Instead, welcoming lawns and yet more flower beds, small groves of many tree types, from elm to Glass Trees and beyond were present, with some hiding the iridescence of peacocks, most prized among visitors being the specially-bred pink and yellow variety.

Unsurprisingly, scattered between visitors to the gardens were guards both in armour and without, stationed to protect not only the magnificent birds but to keep a close watch on the people themselves.

He quickened his step to reach the lawns, and drifted into a grove where he resembled a labourer only to exit as Cimebo the nobleman – at least, according to those who saw him, those whose minds were simply never going to be strong enough to pierce the gift of his illusions. Cimebo ought to still have been travelling the north, and so Thorn entered the palace proper and stopped before the first guard house with its ornate crest of Wings, these painted in magnificent red.

There, he motioned for one of the soldiers to attend. The fellow rose from his seat and stepped quickly. "My Lord?"

"Send a message to Lord Onga and General Tahbe – the King requires their presence in the solarium."

"At once." The guard hurried back inside and Thorn continued toward his destination, south of the palace.

Thorn produced one of only two skeleton keys in existence, using it to enter through a servant's door. In the hall, he paused to ensure he was alone before assuming the mantle of his greatest lie – King Mutolo now strode the fine stone halls in his red and gold.

He passed generous windows, potted plants of vibrant green, and here in the southern wing, a mixture of sculptures stolen from Takirov or soft paintings of cities and deserts, taken from Cresideth. Perhaps images of so much sand and rugged plains with their spiralling trees made for a fitting approach to the sunroom?

A fitting choice by one King or another, at least.

The solarium stood large and clear, constructed with mostly thin, steel lines to support all the glass, shaped as an eight-sided gem. At a glance, it could have been a greenhouse but inside were mostly chairs, divans and small tables, all focused around a pool for swimming. It was perfectly round, tiled with marble and gold, giving the impression of flaming water.

A pair of ladies-in-waiting had removed their shawls and

sat with bare shoulders and heads together at the pool's edge, voices lowered.

"My dears, I will require this room for a time," he said as he entered.

One stood with a little squeak. "Your Majesty!"

He waved a hand. "You have done nothing wrong."

"Thank you, Sire."

Together, they snatched up their clothing and scurried for the exit. One nearly tripped over a chair leg. He held in a sigh, then found one of the chairs that faced the entry, settling into the wooden slats designed with enough give to adjust to his body. Better than heavy cloth options, though anything would work for sun-bathing.

A shame I won't have enough time.

"Ibila," he whispered, waiting for the Twining. "I have called for Onga and Tahbe. Search Onga's room while he is distracted, in case he has yet one more thing up his sleeve."

You are certainly being thorough, she said. *And by the way, thank you for letting me know you had returned.*

"I will make it up to you."

Ah, something for me to look forward to, at last, Your Majesty.

"You're not enjoying all the sneaking around to ferret out secrets?"

Just because I was good at something yesterday, doesn't mean I yearn for it today.

"I will let you focus on your work, then, my loyal subject."

She did not answer, but there might have been just a hint of some grumbling caught upon the Twining that connected them. He smiled, tapping the chair now. Ibila was a gift unlooked for and one he did not deserve.

When Lord Onga and General Tahbe arrived, within moments of one another, Thorn greeted them with a smile. Or, at least from their viewpoint, their *king* did so. "Please, be seated with me."

"Your Majesty." Tahbe nodded as he took a chair opposite, his muscled arms seemingly large enough to toss the piece of furniture through the special Coral Glass.

Lord Onga hesitated a moment before seating himself beside the general, his thin face bearing a recent cut from shaving; he'd been interrupted, perhaps. "How might we serve you, King Mutolo?"

Thorn produced a small cloth bag, then gently tipped the contents into his palm – the ruby stallion with its golden mane and Io, the master-artist's seal, seared into the bottom. "I know you have been worried about the state of the treasury, considering the delays with the nearly completed Coral Tree."

Both men had wide eyes, and Onga's mouth was open. He shut it with a murmur. "This is… The *Charger* was lost last century."

"No longer. And I do believe a certain collector will be most interested in it – no doubt he will offer the crown a more than fair sum."

"Your Majesty…"

"And considering such a windfall, I assume you no longer have any need to petition others behind my back – your concerns can now be funded, in addition to my own, I think you'll find."

Lord Onga wore no smile, but General Tahbe was nodding. "This is most fortunate, Your Majesty."

"Yes."

Onga cleared his throat. "While I am overjoyed, I must say that I have not –"

"To hear that you are overjoyed is wonderful," Thorn replied, dismissing the man's words with a wave of his hand. "Now, I will ensure the western farms are taken care of in your absence, so please do not worry yourself."

Now the man shrank back. "My absence?"

"While you take time to consider your loyalty to the kingdom, I am moving you to more utilitarian quarters in the dungeon." He looked to Tahbe. "General, would you escort our friend as you leave?"

"As you command," the General said as he rose, staring down at Onga.

Meekly, the man rose, starting for the door only to pause before he'd exited, glancing over his shoulder. "I fear you misunderstood me, Your Majesty."

"And I fear I did not – convince me otherwise when I come to visit you, Lord Onga."

Tahbe prodded the man out the door.

Thorn sat back, weighing the Charger in one hand as he lowered his voice. "Ibila, watch Tahbe for me. He's delivering Onga from the solarium to the dungeon."

Having doubts about the general now?

"Being thorough. And I want to know what, if anything, they discuss."

On my way. Where will you be?

"I have something to sell, but after a quick visit to the Coral Tree, you will have all my attention."

CHAPTER 4. – ANYO

The Garden City of Omaila had not changed. Nor would it.

Anyo managed not to sneer as he led Han and Katonga along leafy streets, late-afternoon sun lingering. *Why would this place change?* The colour and variety of the leaves and petals were complimentary, even trampled by passing feet and hooves or wheels from local wagons and travellers alike, a pleasant mix of green, gold and also, in just the right intervals, pink and lavender too. Designed to lull all who witnessed the place into a false sense that such beauty was actually able to penetrate the stone walls and into the dark hearts within.

He nearly chuckled at himself. *That's bitter, even for me.*

The thin gauze of loveliness was echoed in small garden squares with benches and arching branches that surrounded the occasional Guiding Stones. Such glass domes were made from the same durable and impressive mix of Coral and glass used in the palace windows, and while visitors chiefly used the Guiding Stones, locals often flocked to peer down at the magical city maps.

But whenever Anyo saw one, a friend's broken tooth and a smear of blood that had covered the surface came to mind.

Poor Zanal. *How many years ago was that now? Already seven?*

Han gestured to the row of taverns and inns that dotted the thoroughfare, their own rooftop gardens sending greenery down to curl around the windows. From the gardens, laughter echoed. "Want to try House Stag again?"

"Wasn't so bad last time," Katonga added.

Anyo glared across at the row. Buildings dedicated to Stag house, smaller homes with a butcher between, then another merchant, this time a shop that sold only kitchenware… and it, too, bearing the proud crest of the Stag. *Yet the laws state that only inns and taverns can do so.*

In the south of the city, there tended to be less sycophancy toward any single noble house, aside from the Royal House, of course, whose Wings were always well-represented above the doors of inns and taverns.

Not like the eastern ring, which was sometimes jokingly referred to as the Rose quarter, nor the west, which favoured two of the larger houses… when it came to numbers, at least. But change *was* afoot. When even a smaller house like the Stag was trying to compete, something unsavoury was happening. Assuming that was who led the charge.

Their antler-crests were visible on a nearby bow-maker and a tailor. At least the citizens passing in their colourful garb had not stooped to wearing such crests. But when Anyo glanced down a cross-street, there was another; this time a cobbler bore the antlers!

All against the laws.

Or at least, should have been. *I left and things changed. Maybe I shouldn't be surprised.*

But the shifts seemed awfully swift, especially considering

how infrequently the Royal Council sat to deliberate and deliver. More corruption from the old dullards?

Not surprising, if true.

"Claiming House Stag to be not so bad?" Anyo pointed to a second symbol beneath the Stag crest over the inn's wooden door – that of a single eye; a call to those who believed the king had not been brutal enough against the Takirov. *And worse.* "If that is who they have become, I must disagree."

Han grunted. "Is this city-wide?"

"Let's see at least a little more – risky though it is for me to do so."

"If nothing else, keep your hood up then," Katonga said.

"Right."

Katonga glanced around the street. "If we find nothing suitable, do we sleep rough again?"

Han shrugged. "It won't be so unpleasant."

"It's always a little unpleasant."

Anyo sighed. "We should find a place within the walls. We just need to make sure it's one of the Indifferents. That way, if they recognise me, they won't actually care."

"As you wish, Highness."

Anyo groaned, but at least Han had kept his voice low. "And none of that, Han. Especially here."

Thankfully, it did not take long to find an Indifferent – no crest above its simple door and a welcoming scent drifted from the windows of its second storey. Perhaps a bakery above? An unusual mix, but worth trying.

Inside, similar to the streets beyond, no sign of soldiers or guards or of nobles that might recognise him.

Yet without the option of being served in one of the rooms

they booked, Anyo had to take a corner, seated near a painting of a wolf attacking a writhing serpent, a place at least partially shadowed by the fireplace in the centre of the room. It wasn't much, but lacking any proper screen, at least newcomers wouldn't immediately see him.

He hunched over his drink, a sweet wine of fair vintage, until their meals arrived. They were placed upon the table by a young woman whose step seemed slowed by weariness. She gave him a look of what might have been recognition as she left but did not say anything.

I had better be wrong about her. Anyo sighed as he lifted his fork.

The meal was fowl with green vegetables in a mushroom sauce, far richer and far more welcome than travel rations.

Over the course of their meal, the common room had steadily filled but before he finished, he had to relieve himself. Anyo moved easily between the tables, letting other patrons and servers pass first, offering no reason to be noticed more than anyone else in a room now filled with chattering voices and clinking cutlery.

But he stopped in the dim passage beside the kitchen.

One figure stood over another; a child, half-concealed by oversized clothing where she shrank back against the wall. Her red hair had been cut unevenly and her eyes were wide as they stared at clenched fists that loomed over her.

The one with the threatening stance was familiar... *The young woman who served us.* Her voice was low enough that most words were too quiet to hear, but a few curses were audible. Anyo took a step closer and the server was already hissing, no longer intelligible at all.

She drew her leg back, demanding an answer as she did.

The child shook her head and the young woman swung her foot. Her shoe struck the kid, and the defenceless girl gave a yelp. The server only kicked again. Harder.

Anyo charged.

He caught the young woman by the shoulder and shoved her against the wall. "What do you think you are doing?"

Her eyes grew wide with shock, but it passed when she shouted at him. "Get your hands off me!"

Anyo caught her by the throat and squeezed. "You will leave that child alone."

The young woman beat at his arms but he did not let go, only easing his grip enough that she could breathe. And speak.

"This is none of your business, Beggar Prince!"

Appears she did recognise me. It mattered not one bit. "I disagree."

"You think I'm scared of you? You're nothing in this city!"

He grinned. "And that is exactly why no-one will care when I break your neck. I have no reputation to uphold, none to answer to."

Doubt flickered in her eyes, replacing some of the fury. "Let me –"

"Instead, I give you a promise. I will return to this place. Tomorrow. Next week, in one month, perhaps longer, but you will not know when. And when I do, should there be a single hint of a bruise upon that child's body, I will tear you into pieces myself." Anyo leaned close. "But I will save the first piece so that I can feed it to you before you die." He tightened his grip. "Nod if you understand what I have promised you."

The woman nodded, the movement slight.

Anyo released the server, who slid down to the floor gasping for air.

He turned to kneel before the child, whose eyes were still wide. She was trembling, shrinking back further, and he concealed a flinch and the little stab of pain it caused. *And that's because of your temper, fool.* "I will stop her forever, if she does that again."

The child did not answer, only hid her face.

Anyo sighed as he rose and started back down the passage toward the common room. It was time to leave. Not in the least because two of the cooks had appeared at the doorway, peering around the frame.

"You're wrong about this place." The serving girl's voice followed him, uneven, shaky. "We remember what you did. Everyone hates you, Beggar Prince. They'll come for you."

He glanced over his shoulder. "Good luck to them."

At the table, he motioned to Han and Katonga, nodding to the door. They set their cutlery down and as he stood, Katonga took a final drink.

Outside, Anyo frowned as he led them along darkening streets and through thinning crowds toward the east – toward the Royal Quarter.

"Something happen back there?" Han asked.

"It did," he said, pausing at an intersection of four roads with a large, gleaming Guide in its centre. There, a group of the Fiodan stood discussing their path; travelling clerics in their feathered cloaks. "Someone was beating a child. My temper got the better of me, I admit."

"Sounds justifiable," Katonga said with a shrug.

Han frowned. "Only if they're alive."

"She is."

"Very well. So, you roughed her up and she recognised you, is that it? That why we're heading for the Royal Quarter?"

"We are."

"Inevitable, I suppose."

Han was right. *And let's hope I'm not making another mistake.* "Once word spreads that I've returned, I want to be hidden somewhere they won't expect me to be found. We need time to contact Binya. House Stag and the Indifferent inns are a little too obvious now. My family won't expect me to actually hide amongst them."

"Probably not," Han said with a grunt. "But won't it be too hard to stay hidden long enough?"

Anyo hesitated. "Perhaps."

"What about Wisteria?" Katonga suggested. "If we want 'unexpected' and 'difficult to find', I think that would qualify."

"Interesting," Anyo replied. House Wisteria wasn't so antagonistic toward his father as the Rose, but they were no friends to the royals either. *Not unlike me, in that respect.* "How would we gain admittance?"

"We don't have much to offer," Han replied. He scratched at his beard. "Over a year without coming home, searching, sleeping in the wilds and gaining little. It's taken a toll."

"I have information."

Silence met his words.

Anyo glanced between them both. For a long time now, they'd stood by him. Han alone since childhood, and Katonga for a shorter span but with no less devotion. Both believed in his quest, in changing the nation for the better... but their doubts were clear. "Obviously, you do not approve."

Katonga spread his hands. "Well..."

"Am I not already outcast? Despised? On my way to actually employ a Takirov corpse-singer? What is one more transgression to me now?"

Han narrowed his eyes. "You wanted to restore the honour of your House, to unite your siblings under the lost blade and its power. That dream dies if you do this."

"My goal has not changed. And not every secret is protected by the Inner Covenant. I can sell them simple information pertaining to trade deals, perhaps. Or maybe even gambling debts. Gods know there are enough to choose from."

He exhaled. "I see your point but I still don't like it, Your Highness."

And yet, I don't think I care anymore. I cannot fail again. "Whatever the result, the first hurdle is getting them to even meet with us."

CHAPTER 5. – ANYO

House Wisteria's finest inn bore walls draped in purple blossoms, and it stretched across an entire block. Three-storeys tall, it seemed more a mansion of stone with wooden embellishments, than an inn.

So well-lit by torches, lamps and a warm glow from the windows that the carvings of leaping wolves on the windowsills were clear, even upon window boxes too. Statues mounted within alcoves in the stone walls were also featured, most of heroes or patron-nobles, their features cast in sharp relief by the lamps.

Unlike most inns, a spacious entryway greeted Anyo when he led the others inside.

Lined by signs arranged at eye-level, each one described different rooms with their specific menus. A luxury only to be found in Omaila. And few were the inns large enough to offer multiple common rooms for dining, in addition to accommodation, stable and, of course, a gambling den – marked by coloured lamps of blue at the mouth of the stairs.

Only Wisteria House boasted so many.

And it was not just the three entire rooms focused on

Nasaru cuisine of meat, deserts and fish, but the Takirov menu with their spices and sweet, coastal fruits, along with Cresideth and Senoja options too. If the military standing of the Wisteria could not compete with the royals or House Bear, few could match its culinary delights, especially at the Delight of Nations.

Not that Anyo had ever eaten here. Even as a youth, when he first dared to rebel. He folded his arms. *Too busy doing what was best for the family, right? For appearances. For Father.*

When one of the no less than *three* available attendants approached from the long desk, the fellow first brushing imaginary dust from his pink coat, it was with a smile that faltered once he stood close enough.

Anyo sighed, not bothering to hide his displeasure. *Either he thinks our clothes are too shabby or he recognises me.*

"Forgive me, but the suitably polite greeting for a former prince escapes me," the attendant said. "Do you come with an invitation to eat here, sir? Or perhaps a request to do so?"

"A request to speak with the Lord of the House, in fact," Anyo replied. "I bring information that Lord Garakatka would find interesting."

"Ah, I see." The man hesitated. Did he consider calling for guards? Or was it the desire to find a superior, someone upon whose shoulders the responsibility of a potentially difficult decision might be safely conferred upon? Failing that, the fellow was probably weighing up the consequences of turning away an opportunity his master might actually welcome. "I would be happy to make such enquires on your behalf. If you would wait in the sitting room, I will make sure you have something to drink."

"I appreciate that."

The attendant showed them to a small room, which he unlocked with a promise to deliver their request as soon as possible. He gestured within, to five chairs of startling white arranged around a small table. Almost before Anyo had settled into the soft fabric, a young Takirov boy dressed in pink with brown trim entered, carrying drinks upon a tray. He did not speak as he placed the three wines onto the table, only nodded and then left.

Anyo sipped from his glass, a fruity flavour, then leant back in the chair. "Almost a shame we cannot take a meal here too."

"If we end up imprisoned by Garakatka, we'll take many a meal in this place," Han replied as he paced before one of the menus that hung from the wall. "He has a reputation for being rather cunning."

"No. I've made the right choice here, Han. I know it's a gamble, but it's going to pay off. I can feel it."

"Hmmm."

The wait began to stretch on, but when footsteps once again approached the room, Anyo stood, joined by Han and Katonga.

The door opened and a tall, slender man in a black jacket and shirt of pale blue slid into the room, his short hair and beard a lighter brown than most. Lord Garakatka. And while he was no sapling, his build seemed more befitting a dancer than a warrior. Even so, such was not his reputation – he was known as an extremely accomplished duellist.

But Garakatka was not armed, instead entering with a drink of his own and a calm smile. "Welcome to the Delight of Nations," he said as he took a seat, and waved Anyo back into his own. "Please be at ease. Now, it is with some surprise but limited time only that I'm receiving you, of course, and so let me be blunt. Are you truly so bitter about your downfall that you wish to betray your own family?"

Blunt indeed. Anyo shrugged. "You're assuming this is the first time."

The slender fellow raised an eyebrow. "My, my. And what is it that my family can supposedly do for you, Prince Anyo, should I desire the information you have come to offer?"

"I would ask that you bring me the corpse-singer Binya and then arrange for us to leave the city once more, without being noticed."

"Is that truly all?"

"Yes."

Lord Garakatka took a sip from his glass – not wine, but a golden liquor. "This is all very intriguing. Your search for the Sothalic, then?"

"Related to that search, yes."

"Very well." He leant closer. "Tempt me with whatever you can offer."

Anyo placed his hands together. "First, what assurances do I have that you will honour your word and offer the aid we seek?"

The man bristled.

"You were more than willing to deal in blunt words mere moments before, My Lord," Han said.

"A fair observation, I must concede," he replied with a nod. "Obviously, I offer my word now but I will also send for Binya immediately, as a gesture of goodwill." The lord then called for a servant and asked for Binya to be summoned. "Now, please, it is time to reveal your hand."

Anyo leant forward. "One of my brothers, Yonala, owes House Stag debts for Black Coral, something I doubt even Father is aware of. It would be easy to use that against him. Perhaps even buy out the debt if you wanted."

Garakatka set his drink down with a grin. "Fascinating, indeed. And that *is* certainly of use to me. You have my thanks, Highness. And more – as promised, I will arrange for a carriage and escort for this very night."

"I look forward to that."

"While we wait, there is someone who I believe would enjoy a moment with us."

Anyo glanced to the door. While word of his return may or may not have spread through certain parts of the city already, surely not so far as the palace? Few others within the city itself would care enough to seek him out in any event... *Has someone followed me here?* "Who might that be?"

"Your sister."

CHAPTER 6. – MEI

The next town was no bigger than the last, though it had more homes built of stone. Mamalo did not stay long – less than half the morning, selling his spices, bottled foods and smaller items like nails and bolts.

Mei mostly kept out of sight in the back... and boredom followed when she wasn't helping, which was ridiculous in light of the possible danger she faced. But earlier in the day, there had been an older woman who started shouting at Mamalo upon seeing Mei carrying wares to his long folding table. It was almost enough to have her drop a particularly valuable piece of artwork – something from Takirov: paper bark created to appear as a horse and carriage, something that took months to create.

And the few times she did venture out afterwards, it was impossible not to feel the woman's gaze from across the street, glaring from where she leant against her front door.

So, it was with a weight lifted that they set out once more. She nearly asked Mamalo about the woman but if the old bird mistook her for Senoja, that was probably explanation enough.

On they travelled through the last of the morning and

into the afternoon, passing travellers or smiling farmers in dirty clothes, many wearing straw hats. But what caught her eye most were not the clothes themselves, which were not so different from items worn in Nokema, it was the little crests sewn into cloaks or tunics. They were not worn by all of the folk they passed, but plenty bore them. Most crests were of a bear's head like the inn, and only once she saw a duel axe blade.

Despite her curiosity, she did not know how to ask Mamalo about them.

It wasn't until a cold moon lit the road that they reached another campsite. There, she once again attended to the wards and then collected firewood. After, she ate hot stew that was a little too salty for her liking, before seeking her bedroll in the rear of the wagon.

And so, the same routine held over the days until they reached the town nearest Giloam – which she had learned was called Cangola – and where, supposedly, she would find someone she could speak with. Or to. Or who could speak *for* her? Translate on behalf of her Nasaru guide? *Anything to help, I hope.*

While most of her doubts about Mamalo had eased, new tension was taking its place, lingering in her shoulders and chest whenever she lifted her flask to drink. Would Cangola hold even more threats? Giloam sounded as though it would be a large place. *Surely that means there'll be more soldiers. More suspicious eyes upon me.*

When they reached Cangola, the differences were easy enough to spot. It boasted a large wooden wall, and though it was empty of guards, narrow slots were visible at regular intervals. *For watchers?*

Inside, the stone buildings with their red roof-tiles were built closer than in the villages. Many were bigger too, with a second floor, making them taller than the dome of the village Oratory. And set above the doors or sometimes windows were more signs and plaques. Most were of the bear's head, though some showed three feathers. *Different again from the lone traveller who bore axe blades.*

Here, the people did not dress so differently to anything else she'd seen in Nasaru so far, save for a pair walking in blue and purple silks. Two younger folks followed behind in plainer attire, arms laden with goods… and by their expression, they did not seem to be helping out of any willingness. *Lords and servants, based on Denuko's descriptions, at least.* Though if Anyo had been a lord, then he certainly did not match what she saw now.

And while Mei received her share of dark looks from those who passed their wagon, most did not seem interested enough to even turn their heads from their business or conversations. The crowds were a steady flow too – the first part of the stone-paved town could have contained the whole of Nokema.

Most surprising, were a few weavings and blankets from home, arranged for sale at a stall in a large market square… but she did not ask to examine them, instead asking Mamalo if they were close to whomever could help.

Mamalo nodded, then pointed ahead.

The wide street branched before an odd, two-storey building with a somewhat triangular front. Twin doors rested on either side, along with large, regularly-spaced windows. To the right, the paved street rose up toward a walled mansion whose roof had been mounted with large bows. A gentle slope on the left ended in a wide circle of smaller homes, some with missing glass in the windows, bearing makeshift repairs instead, boards or sometimes blankets.

Nestled within those poorer homes rested a small open area with a two-storey building, its pale walls reflected in mirror-like puddles from last night's rain. The walls of this building were clad with… something. Or perhaps they had been painted white? But more striking was the large sign above the doorway, which was of two hands pressed together – shimmering in silver.

Three youths sat before the mysterious building – two girls and a boy, each with similar features, and one whose arm was bandaged.

Was that the place Mamalo had pointed to?

The merchant turned the wagon down the slope, answering her question. He stopped before the white walls with a little nod of what seemed to be satisfaction, before climbing down.

Based on the injured boy, had Mamalo taken her to a place for healing? Mei joined the merchant and gestured to the silver hands, projecting her thoughts now. *Is it a healer that can help somehow?*

"Yes." He replied in Nasaru, one of the few words she now understood, as he attended to the horse. He then lifted his purse and glanced inside before drawing the string closed once more and entering the healer's building.

Mei followed Mamalo, ignoring the stares from the youngest girl. The girl whispered about how pale Mei's skin was, quickly being admonished by her elder sister. *I suppose they've never seen someone like me before.*

The entryway bore twin staircases and branching corridors

lined with open doors, the ends of beds visible within. The only other furniture inside was a pair of desks, one more of a wide table draped in grey cloth. A man in a shapeless smock sat at the second desk behind that table. He was unpacking rolls of bandages from a box and writing in a ledger; the gentle scratch of his quill almost lost beneath some musical instrument heard from above... perhaps stringed, like a more delicate version of the lute from home.

The man stood with a welcoming smile. Mei let Mamalo speak, and very quickly they were shown to a bright room lit by large windows where green, flowing plants were almost aglow. Inside, a patient lay abed – her brow was creased, but the pain must not have been overwhelming, since she smiled back at the woman who attended her.

The healer?

She could have been from Nokema... did that make her Senoja?

The woman was tall with green eyes and dark hair cut short, and her clothing was more fitted than her helper. It also bore a waxy sheen. *For what purpose?* But perhaps it ought to have been obvious: *to make it easier to wash off blood.*

After a moment, the healer stepped aside, scroll in hand, to greet Mamalo and Mei too.

Mamalo and the healer spoke pleasantly enough at first, but once he offered her coin for something, she frowned and made a gesture that might have meant 'not enough' or simply 'no'. Whatever it was, things did not seem to be going well. And there was nothing Mei could do to help.

Mamalo gestured to Mei as he continued to speak. The healer regarded her with doubt at first but something like interest appeared to take hold.

But what was being said? Were things about to become dangerous?

Mei readied to strike, just in case. Yet the conversation seemed to be taking a turn for the better. The healer shrugged, then gestured to the money and tilted her head back to the hallway. She strode out, and Mamalo followed, smiling at Mei as he motioned for her to join them.

Is she going to help?

Mamalo offered her the only word she knew. "Yes."

CHAPTER 7. – MEI

In the next room, this one empty of patients, the healer stood before a locked box of steel. The box rested upon a stone table between the woman and Mei, with Mamalo waiting close by. He had introduced the healer, Katharin, and tried to explain *how* she would help, but even with Mei asking a range of questions, it was unclear.

It did seem that the woman was going to offer some *thing* that might make a difference. A magical item perhaps?

Katharin withdrew a key from a small pouch upon her belt and unlocked the box, then lifted a second, smaller box free. It was one of many boxes inside the first, each marked with Nasaru symbols, but the final blue box the healer held was unmarked. Inside it in turn, rested a single bone carving – a tiny flower bud. Katharin lifted the carving free and turned it over, revealing a small spike.

The healer then lifted the carving to her ear... then pointed to Mei.

What does this mean? What is that?

And while both Mamalo and Katharin heard her, neither answered at once, the merchant rubbing at his chin. Katharin mimed driving the bone into her own earlobe and Mei flinched. *Why?*

The healer paused, raising her hands with a gentle smile as she spoke, her tone soothing. The words were, of course, meaningless, but the woman was certainly making no threatening moves. And supposedly the item would help?

Katharin snapped her fingers as she straightened. Next, she raised the bone to her ear but turned so that she faced Mei side-on. This concealed the item from Mei's view, and the woman began to mouth words – not actually speaking.

She then turned, still facing side-on, but now the bone was visible to Mei. Once more, the healer mimed the act of pushing the bone carving into her earlobe, and then spoke aloud, meeting Mei's gaze as if to check that she understood.

Mei nodded slowly… perhaps she did.

The little performance meant that Mei would be able to understand others, if she had the bone in her ear. *I hope that's what it means.*

Mei moved forward to examine the sharp point when Katharin held the earring out on her palm. She lifted the bone and touched it with her finger, only gently. How much would it hurt going into her ear?

If I use this, I'll be able to understand you?

Katharin nodded, then put a hand on her shoulder. Once more, the woman spoke words that were no doubt meant to be comforting. The healer unhooked a small pouch from her belt and removed a dark leaf from within. She folded the leaf, rubbing it between thumb and forefinger. An earthy scent rose and the healer lifted her hand to rub it upon Mei's earlobe.

A slight sting followed but did not last.

Katharin waited a moment, then lifted a hand to her own ear, flicking her lobe – then gestured for Mei to repeat the action.

Mei did so. Twice, just to be sure she'd felt nothing at all. Whatever the leaf had been, it wasn't so different from wolfspaw in Nokema.

I see. The numbness will stop the pain.

A nod.

And the bone is magic.

Once again, Katharin nodded, this time with a smile. She handed Mei the bone in its flower bud shape. It was remarkable. Somehow, such a tiny thing would make understanding an entire new language possible. What other astonishing things could the sorcerers of Nasaru do? Somehow, fed by the magical Black Coral…

Mei set the point against her ear… or thought she did, but she couldn't be certain. *I don't want to miss.*

Katharin took over, acting carefully as she inserted the bone into Mei's lobe. Some discomfort followed, but nothing too painful at all. Mei raised a hand to check for blood, but her ear was dry.

Does it work right away? Mei asked them both.

"Not for ujale," Katharin replied. "For some nannaw, not at all."

Oh… I understood most of that!

Mamalo grinned. "That's a relief, I rasq eb hanelo."

I got some of that too.

The healer leant against the wall and while she did not seem displeased at all, her smile had faded, as though she were simply a serious person perhaps. "It might take several days before you safutetta everything, but it's working much faster than I garu."

Mei turned to Mamalo. *Thank you for doing this, Mamalo.*

"Of course."

But this must be an incredibly priceless thing. Mei touched the bone. *I don't know how I could repay you. Either of you.*

Katharin reached up to pat Mamalo upon the cheek. "Don't worry. He's happy to raise his ongmariw to the yasbe."

The merchant shrugged.

"Not to mention the eb kadabul favour he now owes me."

"My pleasure, Lady Katharin," he replied, though his tone suggested at least a little sarcasm.

I have to do something – I have a debt to you both.

Katharin glanced at Mamalo. "Well?"

The merchant cleared his throat. "Now that we can speak more isinah, I do have a request. Something I have wanted to ask since we met."

What is it?

"I want your help negotiating a trading deal with Senoja."

Mei blinked. *That was... unexpected.*

And most utterly impossible. She kept her thoughts to herself. *Even if I could fool the Senoja... I can't negotiate; I don't know anything about trading!* How long would such a task even take? *There's no time to travel into Senoja. Even if I find Iggy first, it would be too dangerous.* Was the only available option to lie? To pretend she would be useful? After Mamalo had helped her, protected her, spent his money and grown indebted to others on her behalf... even knowing that he had expected her help from the beginning did not make it easier to lie.

"I will handle the actual negotiating," he said, only partially guessing the cause of her hesitation.

Little choice. *I will do my best. Provided it does not take me too far from my path.*

The merchant smiled. "That's wonderful. And I have no afwarme, in truth. Let us see what the oau-sorcerers of Giloam have to say first."

"If you expect to reach the city before midnight, you should leave soon," Katharin observed.

Thank you, again, Mei said as the woman showed them back into the halls and to the entryway. Mamalo nodded for Mei to wait outside a moment. "I will join you soon," he said.

Outside, she smiled down at the children, who grinned back. It did not take long before Mamalo returned to the wagon. She waved to the children and joined the merchant upon the seat.

Once more, they rolled over the cobbles, where they soon passed a figure wearing a feathered robe and carrying a staff. The man wore a kind expression but what caught her attention was the staff. Carved from a dark wood, it appeared as though a snake was coiled there, its head peering out.

Just as Denuko described, the man had to be one of the Fiodan.

She glanced over her shoulder as they passed.

He didn't seem to be carrying a lot of medicines...

Soon enough, the wagon was leaving not just the poorer area but the town itself, passing through wooden gates and heading back onto the highway.

At one point, Mei looked behind, but the walls of Cangola were already growing small. The land around the road remained if not empty, far closer to barren than it had on the eastern side of the town.

Here, the earth was becoming stonier, the sparse grass and spiky shrubs darker. Stands of trees were few and far between, though the same old river was not too far distant, like a blue serpent and now known as River Waafir. It continued west and would eventually pass mountains that divided the western part of Nasaru and Senoja from each other, something she had learned from one of Mamalo's maps.

And while the precious bone earring could not help her read the Nasaru script, the merchant had explained something about their location and his intended destination for trading, a city not so far beyond the border, one that was supposedly eager for his merchandise.

But it was Giloam that she asked most about, and the oau-sorcerers. Oau, Mei had learned, meant 'coral'.

"You must have lived a quiet life, even in your village," he said. "Not to know much about the sorcerers."

She glanced away. *Well, I know that they use Black Coral and they can do all kinds of things.*

"Some of them can," he replied. "Arts of healing, war and scrying are most common."

What about in Giloam? Is there someone there skilled enough to help me?

He spread his hands, letting the reins drop into his lap a moment. "It's hard to say. You haven't exactly told me much about who you're looking for. Are they back in the valley? On some island somewhere? There will be plenty of powerful sorcerers in Giloam, but I don't really know their individual limits." He paused. "Many are under direct supervision of the military. All will require significant compensation."

Right. Mei glanced away. *That's an entirely different problem.*

Mamalo smiled. "Not if we can convince the Senoja to trade with us."

I'll do my best.

He gave the reins a light snap and the wagon picked up speed. "First, let's reach Giloam."

Once more, Mamalo rode on into the dark. He seemed confident enough on the road of paved stone that was lit by lanterns hung from the hitching post. And it was by that light that a pair of passing soldiers became visible.

Mei shrunk back in her seat, leaning toward Mamalo's larger frame, but the soldiers in their gleaming armour paid the wagon little heed. Like the last group she saw, they seemed somewhat agitated. Was that simply their nature, as Mikal and the other Elders might have claimed?

A faint but expansive glow soon appeared beyond the crest of a hill. It seemed to be in response to the smaller and brighter glow from homes where they lay in surrounding fields. *Is that Giloam already?* And while the fields seemed healthy enough, animals were absent, not even cows that she'd seen elsewhere in Nasaru seemed present so far.

Instead, smaller shapes grazed within pens near to the roadside. It was possible to catch glimpses of them, but most details were unclear beneath only the newly-risen moon.

When Mamalo stopped the wagon to relieve himself, Mei took a lantern and approached one of the fences to peer closer at the animals. They were dog-like, or even like large foxes, with short brown fur and pointed ears... and their eyes were so black that they swallowed the light, staring up at her from faces lined with rows of sharp teeth.

She stumbled back with a cry. "What are these things?"

Her heart was thumping within her chest.

"Mei?" Footsteps followed Mamalo's voice and then he joined her, eyes wide with concern. "What things?"

She pointed. *Them. The animals.*

"Oh." He chuckled. "I didn't think to mention them. They're called mitiru and they're harmless. They very, very rarely bite."

But they have so many teeth... and their eyes.

He knelt by the fence and reached through the fencing, making soft, soothing sounds as he did. Mei tensed, but the fanged-animal only sniffed at his hand and, apparently finding nothing of interest, moved away to chew upon one of the plants found within the pen.

Mamalo rose. "See?"

But, they look like they'd be vicious.

"They need their teeth to shred the urodi plants – some people like to exaggerate a little and call them leather-plants, actually."

Oh. So, they're not kept for their pelts... but to control the urodi plant?

"Not precisely," Mamalo said as he returned to the wagon. Mei climbed after as he continued. "That's a part of it in some areas, but the farmers harvest the droppings and use it to make a powerful compost..." he trailed off as a frown came over his face.

What's wrong?

"Before, I just realised. I understood you. When you called out, you called them 'things' and I understood your words. Not just in my mind, but I understood your voice too."

Really?

"I did. Can you try it again?"

Mei paused. *I must have used my power at the same time, due to the shock…*

She answered by infusing her words with telepathy – not just thinking while she spoke aloud, not in a casual way, but trying to *push* her thoughts out through her voice at the same time, toward Mamalo.

"How about this?" she asked.

He grinned. "Well, now that you mention it, I actually don't know whether I 'heard' your words in my mind, like usual, or whether I understood your voice, after all. Maybe it doesn't matter?"

She smiled. "Well, if I can get used to this, it might be nice to use my voice more often."

Confusion flickered across Mamalo's face a moment, as if he hadn't understood each word perhaps, but he nodded. "I'll teach you some more, but I'm sure it will be more reliable in time."

"Thank you." *He's probably right.*

And despite the uncertainty of her attempts, there was one obvious positive that she had been reminded of – control of her Inora gifts meant that she could still choose to keep some thoughts private. A good thing, since she had secrets of her own.

CHAPTER 8. – CINDER

Slipping into the Valley had not been too traumatic, despite the Greyshield leaving him very little in order to reach the place to begin with.

It had been no pleasant stroll across sun-dappled fields either.

The highway through the marsh was not always clear or well-maintained, and the insects drove Cinder to the limits of his patience, but at least he faced no barriers, no guards, nor unseen magic to stop him in the end... it was a little confusing.

After all, rumours usually held a grain of truth or two. And stories about the Inora suggested a difficult passage to reach their home.

But if Inora *were* mostly forgotten, why was the road fair enough for wagons? And if the people were so powerful and dangerous, would merchants risk visiting at all? Yet fabrics from Nokema were still seen in markets at times, even commanding a fair price in the capital due to their sturdy weave and long-lasting colours.

He sighed as he turned back to glance toward the strange symbols upon the rock face, ringing the large opening from which he had exited. Of course, the symbols offered no answers. Not now and not as he'd passed into a much gentler shadow cast by pale-blue trees that surrounded the road.

Perhaps I'll find a few answers of my own. Fabrics alone were not enough for most merchants. If the Inora possessed something truly valuable, they would be fending off outsiders. And that was not the case. On the surface of the matter, at least.

Such a thing hardly meant that the villagers didn't have *something* truly special hidden away somewhere.

"They had better be," he muttered. *If not, getting my hands on some food before heading back to the city will have to be enough.*

Cinder strode on, following the road through the forest with its odd, glass-like blossoms until making a cold, reasonably miserable camp in failing light and waiting for sleep.

When dawn came, he rose with it, taking a precious mouthful of his dwindling water supply and travelling on, coming eventually to a grassy plain. There, he found little but the road, markers, and the occasional grasshopper.

By his second nightfall in the valley, little had changed. He was again forced to endure the night wrapped in his cloak, having failed to find anything edible, let alone been able to meet or even *see* another person that might help.

And when he finally reached his destination, stomach aching and the last of his water gone, the dusty path leading to Nokema was empty too – just like the village itself. Or, more accurately, empty of voices or movement. Not even a faint breath of wind stirred bright curtains that lay within the mud brick homes… but dark shapes did rest upon the ground.

He slowed.

The shapes were animals… extremely large cats? Before

he reached the nearest, he paused to glance around but still nothing moved between the circular homes. He reached for a knife – something rusted he'd found within the swamps – though it offered little comfort at the thought of being attacked by such creatures.

He knelt at the corpse. "Well…" The cat's dark fur bore no traces of blood but the torso was bent in half, flies hovering where bile had escaped its large fangs. A paw was broken too, something which somehow drew more attention to its size.

The next body lay within the wreckage of someone's rose hedge, appearing equally broken-jointed.

And it was only one of many scattered about the village.

Even with the apparent lack of human victims, it seemed something quite unpleasant had occurred.

Which means no-one will be lingering.

Cinder skipped across the garden of the nearest home and slipped inside.

A single, large room contained bed, basin and stove, a small table resting beneath one of the windows. Little seemed out of place; the sun-patterned blankets, shelves with utensils arranged in order. A jug of water even sat upon the table. *As though someone had just ducked outside a moment.*

No better time to do a little investigating.

First, he reached for the water and drank, spilling some down his shirt and finishing with a sigh. *Somehow, that's almost better than wine at the Delight of Nations.*

Cinder drifted to a small alcove in the wall where a plain box rested. He lifted the lid on silent hinges, yet inside, nothing but polished stones of varying colours. Next, he searched some of the more obvious places – beneath the mattress, inside a small chest and even checking the undersides of table and chairs, but there was nought of value.

He strode outside and headed for a larger home.

This time, he had to step over the corpse of another oversized cat to enter, where he found blood stains on the floor, along with shattered crockery and a broken chair. But the house had more rooms… and hopefully, more satisfying secrets.

Yet the longer he searched, the less he uncovered; more polished stone and sometimes writings in undecipherable words but nothing else.

Little changed in the next home, not in the fourth either, until he found himself stalking along the decking of the largest building in the village, a domed place that bore multiple entries. *Surely this place has* something *worth hiding away?*

He shoved the nearest door open.

A stretching, empty floor and dais. Upon the dais rested wooden chairs in a half-circle. More of nothing… but behind the chairs, a single door marked with symbol painted in white. "You better be worthwhile," he grumbled as he approached.

A storage room waited beyond, walls lined with rolls of colourful bunting and just beneath the window, a faded flag bearing the Blue Hawk of Senoja. Interesting enough, perhaps, but not so easy to smuggle out of the place, even if it was worth a lot of gold. Which it wasn't. *And honestly, I deserve something far better after what I've been through lately.*

Hope flared at a small row of chests. They had been arranged beneath more shelving, these lined with jars bearing bold labels. He slid forward to kneel before the row and smiled, patting the lid of one chest – the one that was locked. "I'm expecting fine things, now," he told it.

His lock-picking tools came to hand swiftly and he got to work, curbing his impatience by counting to one hundred in intervals of five, and soon enough, hinges squeaked open.

A single blade.

The weapon lay upon folded cloth of a dark hue that heightened its silver. It had been engraved with interlocking lines and featured a small, circular hole near the hilt. When he lifted the dagger, there seemed to be just a hint of white to the steel. Quite unusual.

And hopefully quite the antique. It was exactly the sort of thing collectors in Omaila would squabble over. The question of exactly how valuable did remain, but finally, *finally*, something worth stealing.

The blade's edge sliced through the cloth, which he used to wrap the handle, sheathing the antique with a nod. Then he placed his rusty weapon inside and closed the lid, locking it before moving on to the next chest.

Voices drifted near.

Cinder hesitated, hand outstretched. Were they going to enter the dome? He rose and slipped from the room, pressing himself against a wall to listen.

Unfamiliar words reached him as twin sets of footfalls crossed the decking... and began to fade. The villagers, or whoever was outside, were moving beyond the domed building. They did not sound hurried, either. Perhaps now was a fine time to ingratiate himself with the locals? *Quite a long road back to the city without supplies.*

By now, it also seemed clear that danger from the attack had passed.

He crossed the empty floor, following the voices to the

nearest exit, where he paused before creeping into the street. Ahead, two men in green robes walked a narrow path leading from the village. The sleeves on their robes did not pass far beyond the elbows, revealing pale skin, very much like the Senoja. Their hair was pale too, one short and greying and the other's more blond, reaching his shoulders.

They carried shovels on their way, heads swivelling to keep a close watch on the surrounding trees, with additional attention spent on a slope that led down to golden fields of wheat. Plenty of the stalks were broken there, flattened in places with more than a few dark shapes prone upon the earth.

More dead cat-monsters, most likely.

"This has become a dangerous place to visit, stranger."

Cinder spun at the heavily-accented voice.

The Inora were facing him now, the older one leaning on his shovel. Neither glared in anger, but a tension filled the air. They held a power ready, as if an unseen blow could land at any moment.

"Forgive my intrusion," Cinder said, raising his hands.

"Perhaps we may."

"I am not here to commit violence. I am merely a traveller. I barely survived the marsh and I'm seeking help from any who might offer it."

The Inora conferred a moment, their words certainly at least similar to those spoken in Senoja. After a time, the younger nodded. Yet once more, it was the older fellow who answered. "You may not find much assistance here, but should you survive the next attack, we will try to help you."

CHAPTER 9. – ROKURA

Rokura tossed his apple core through the open window and into the garden then slumped back into the armchair, letting its wings support his head as he closed his eyes. It was not in contentment but a growing frustration. "There is something we haven't considered, Cosequ, but to be honest, it just doesn't add up either way."

His cousin waved a beckoning hand. "Happy to hear it."

Rokura lowered his voice; of the few he truly trusted, Cosequ was one. "What if the Duke's movements were not wholly connected to Brutan and the other rebels? Or at least, not *only* connected to the abduction of Asaro."

"Assuming they succeeded in finding him. Or aren't returning, having mistaken someone else for Asaro."

"Yes."

"Well, it's not implausible..." He lifted the command post's own logbook. "You think that's why troops were moved through in smaller, unassuming groups? A supporting force of Nasaru traitors for the rebels?"

"Considering the time span, why not? That way at least, the Takirov would have a sizable, entirely legitimate-seeming escort waiting, should they need it."

Cosequ rose and strode to the opposite window. He frowned down at the training yard. "If that's true, what are we going to do about it?"

"We?"

He chuckled. "You don't want my help?"

Rokura shook his head. "I assumed I'd continue tracking them, and you'd handle Governor Conisz, finding more evidence on this side of the border."

"I'll leave Lieutenant Kini in charge of that – she's capable enough, believe me."

"And the garrison?"

"Cehwo is another entirely capable soldier," Cosequ replied with a grin. "So, how about it, cousin? Want to save the kingdom together?"

Rokura laughed. "Shouldn't I be offering for *you* to join *me*?"

"Most likely."

"Then have you already thought ahead to when we catch up to a force of that size, in Takirov?"

His cousin raised a finger. "I have. Princess Kiteka is in Atanoph for negotiations; she will have a retinue and can, of course, commandeer any garrison she might require."

That *was* something. "Provided Brutan has taken them near enough to strike. They could be farther south by now." Rokura produced the wooden disc from an inner pocket. It still indicated a southern location. "All I can be sure of is that they're still travelling south."

"Good enough for the moment," Cosequ replied. "And don't forget your mysterious friend."

Rokura stood, joining his cousin to look across the dry yard where Iggy sat astride a horse, reins gripped hard. Prime Scout Lettaka was urging the lad to relax, a gentle smile upon his face. "The horse can feel your tension," he was saying, his voice audible enough.

"The lad is certainly powerful… in a way that seems quite different from other Senoja," Cosequ said.

"Yes. I'm not sure we can rely on his power to be consistent, however." He sighed. Iggy still had not been able to explain exactly how he had arrived at the ruins in a burst of light, but it was a blessing in any event. "Or maybe I just think that because *I* don't understand it."

"But you're planning on helping him, aren't you?"

Rokura nodded. *Somehow.*

"Then there's no harm in using his power in exchange. He's offered as much."

"Hmmm."

"That sounds like it's settled to me." Cosequ smacked a fist into his palm. "I'll organise our mounts and provisions. Give me some time to arrange everything else with my seconds, then it's time to hunt some traitor-scum."

"And save those under our care, remember?" Rokura added as he gathered his own belongings and started for the yard.

"Of course."

Outside, Rokura approached Iggy, boots stirring faint trails of dust.

Are we leaving now? Iggy asked as he dismounted, managing to do so without becoming tangled in the stirrups as he had upon his first attempt.

"Soon, yes. You seem a little more at ease here."

Iggy had already raised his hood, and he faced the horse.

A little.

"You'll grow accustomed the longer you ride," he said. "Like most skills, really."

I hope that's true.

Rokura reached out to pat the horse's neck. The mount seemed restless, waiting for Lettaka to return with food perhaps. "Are you still set on seeking out the Mistress of Obsidian?"

I am.

"I cannot promise I can guide you there, protect you *and* chase down the rebels all at once," Rokura said. "There may be a time when I must choose."

I don't expect you to give up your quest. If you can get me to Atanoph at least, I will definitely appreciate it.

He sighed. Convincing the lad was useless but he had to try at least once more. "I fear she may be a match even for your impressive powers."

Supposing she is real. She is meant to be over two hundred years old and made from obsidian? It does not ring true, surely?

"Nor would your abilities, if I described them to another."

Iggy gave a slight shrug.

"Then let me share a tale I recall from my youth – that of the twenty-six Black Coral Sorcerers who set out to destroy her after a plague, and the one woman who returned."

They blamed her for the plague?

"People often blame what they do not understand on convenient targets, so I would not be surprised if she were not responsible at all. History texts are not clear."

I see.

"Kiroba, the strongest, was the one who led and the only

one to survive. When she returned, she crawled from a maw of fire, barely breathing when the villagers found her. At first, for weeks, she could not speak – she could only breathe, only cling to life. Her entire body, from her skin right down to her bones, had been drained of near all she required to live, turning her into a white, almost translucent being, one that threatened to fade into the very sheets she lay upon, turning the sun into a curse."

Iggy straightened. *A curse.*

"Yes. For while Kiroba recovered in both mind and body, learning to speak once more, to move her limbs as before, even to use the magic of the Black Coral, she spent the rest of her days in darkness, unable to bear the feel of sunlight. It seared through her pale skin and into her organs and bones. It is said that even reflected light could cause the woman pain." He paused. "Only years after that fateful raid did Kiroba attempt to walk beneath the sun, and that was to save her daughter."

What happened?

"She rescued her child but the sun reduced her to a pile of ash," Rokura replied with a heavy sigh. "I do not know how your body works at all, Iggy, but do you really want to take such a risk? How long could you survive, living in darkness?"

I do not know. He clenched his hands, then looked up at Rokura. *Wouldn't you take any risk if you had been born like this?*

Rokura exhaled. "I won't deny that. I just hope you have some sort of plan. Something more than relying on that... skull. I assume that is where you learned of the Mistress?"

He nodded. *We have to reach the city first and find a clue as to her location.*

"The skull cannot simply tell you?"

I'm not sure if she doesn't actually know, or if Nuka is just testing me.

"I see." Rokura hesitated. The pink skull and its menacing inhabitant – Nuka, it seemed – was still nowhere to be seen, but it was the obvious explanation as to where Iggy had come up with the possibility of seeking out the Mistress. Unfortunately, the lad was touchy when it came to the skull. "What exactly have you been told about a clue in Atanoph?"

Only that it will lead us to her.

"Then you're not certain, yourself?"

No, but I don't have a choice.

CHAPTER 10. – ROKURA

Is there something strange about this place? Iggy asked Rokura as the group of three rode down the dark mountainside, hooves echoing through the Black Coral gullies at a pace that was neither taxing on the horses nor too much trouble for a new rider.

"Long, long ago, these gullies rested beneath the ocean," Cosequ replied.

"What are you detecting?" Rokura asked.

A sense of... of something lingering. Faint. There's something that's still alive about this place.

"It's mostly stone, you know," Cosequ said. "I feel traces of vanished magic... but that is all. Are we in danger?"

That might not be what I'm sensing.

"The only travellers we have passed have been innocuous enough; merchants laden with Black Coral wagons and the like," Rokura added. "Nothing out of the ordinary so far."

Tell me what you see.

Rokura glanced around at the rising walls. Ragged shapes had frozen together to create barriers of twisted stone – or, petrified coral and stone forced together by wind and rain over centuries – and described what he saw as best he could. Over such a long period of time, the place had changed. Small, jag-like openings led deep into the walls and some of the coral stood in shapes more like outlines, frozen in relief.

"Well, the colour is what most travellers remark upon. Pale grey, like charcoal, but threaded within there are hints of shimmering orange and pink, sometimes gold too. You could say that in places, it looks like veins nearing the surface of the walls, other times it's more of a general tint to the stone," he said.

I should have mentioned that I do not understand colours, despite my sister's attempts to help. I see things differently.

"My apologies," Rokura replied. He nearly asked another question about exactly how Iggy perceived the world… but had there been hint of pain in the lad's explanation? No need to dig into a wound.

No, that still helps. I don't think it's the ancient coral that I'm sensing.

"The plants here are not so different," Cosequ added. "Purple shrubs, twisted trees with grey bark, leaves almost… ah, black. Sorry. That probably wasn't much help, was it? Some people say the trunks look like scales, though."

Scales?

"Right. They don't really glitter, they're… dark, too. With tiny flecks of colour that you can scrape off if you try. They're not really useful. Sometimes animals gnaw on them to sharpen their teeth."

Can we stop a moment? I'd like to check the tree trunks.

Rokura tugged on his reins, slowing to a walk. "Why?"

There's something about this place and I think it might be the trees... they could be useful.

"Do you mean...for use in medicines? Or magic? Something like that?"

I don't really know. Touching will help me 'see' it better, you could say.

Cosequ tugged at his braid. "I haven't heard that they're magical, you know. And plenty of sorcerers would have checked over the generations."

But I'm not a sorcerer.

"Then we might as well stop for a bite to eat. See what you can do," Cosequ replied.

Rokura nodded his agreement. "Take some water too, Iggy."

I will.

Rokura leant against a rock formation on the opposite side of the road, watching as Iggy paused before one of the dark trees. Known as *pinrobu-ma* to some, or 'dark hands' if translated to Nasaru, though their formal name escaped him.

Whether they would provide useful or not was yet to be seen, of course. Iggy was now scraping at the bark with his blade, letting the scaly bark fall into his palm. Once he had however much he deemed enough, the lad tipped it into a pocket and returned to his mount to pour a little water into his other palm.

Then he looked up with a small nod. *I don't know how it will be useful yet, but I'm ready to move on if you both are.*

After a quick meal, they rode on, hoof-beats echoing along the highway. And while Rokura led Cosequ and Iggy past travellers on the road, the sun beginning is cool descent, it was difficult not to wonder just how many might have been soldiers playing at being merchants. Or simply spies or smugglers, though most folks were Nasaru.

Whatever Duke Bedoa had in mind, it wouldn't necessarily involve sending anyone along his back trail.

But upon riding through the heavy gates protecting the border town of Oris and into a busy square where they dismounted, a familiar feeling of being watched returned. It wasn't just the stares from Takirov and Nasaru alike – his grey cloak always drew its share of nervous or resentful glances – but a specific watcher. *Half a lifetime spent sneaking about, of living mostly in the shadow between places… well, it at least has the benefit of this sort of awareness.*

Beneath his boots, patterns of paler stone in the cobblestones could be used to guide visitors, something far more common in the south. They arched off from the square in different directions, old, worn runes sending travellers to inns, markets, and healers. And while things had changed over the centuries, left of the square was a row of inns and taverns several streets deep – each bearing the crest of this or that family.

Not unlike Nasaru towns, local lodgings reserved for Greyshields would rest deeper within, but such a place would be a last resort, considering he travelled not alone, but with Cosequ and Iggy.

He glanced across the row of taverns, checking on each window, the narrow openings of alleyways and upon the rooves too. As he searched for the watcher, he spared a thought for Iggy.

The lad wore a face covering, as if unwell, and had his hood pulled forward. He stood between Cosequ and his own mount, keeping his head lowered. *Good lad.* Iggy obviously needed little advice; after all, he'd had to hide himself before. Or, most likely, been fooled by someone bad enough to end up buried.

Rokura paused. *No small feat for him to trust me now then, considering how he was treated before.*

An important fact to keep in mind.

Of the inns, the Panther would have offered Cosequ extra favour but as a Greyshield, all inns were obliged... Still, Stag House at the end of the street offered windows on all floors, and a ladder climbing up to the roof on one side of the building.

"We'll impose upon the hospitality of the Stags," Rokura said, and led the way down the street and swiftly to the inn's dim stable.

One of the stable hands, a Takirov lad, wiped sweat from his brow as he greeted them, brush in one hand. "Welcome to the Lion's Table. Let me take your..." he trailed off when he noticed Iggy.

"Our young companion is not well, but so long as he isn't disturbed, none here will face any threat," Cosequ said.

"Oh..."

"You have my guarantee, good fellow," Cosequ added. "Surely you can trust the word of a sorcerer? After all, I am versed in healing arts as well."

The young man nodded slowly. "A separate room for him, then."

"The Greyshields will cover the additional expense," Rokura added.

"Our thanks," he said with a quick bow. "If you'll leave your mounts to me, simply take the door by the water barrels and speak with Yiri. She will arrange for your rooms."

Rokura led them to the entryway, pausing to let a patron

leave – a fellow in pink and red satin, who quickened his step as he headed for the horses.

What's a lion? Iggy hadn't looked up, hadn't changed his posture at all, but his curiosity had obviously been strong enough to ask.

Rokura glanced down. *Considering the complete lack of reaction from both Cosequ and that patron exiting the inn, that was a question just for me.* Meaning Iggy could be selective about whose mind he sent his thoughts into.

"Let's find a room and I'll do my best to describe one."

"One what?" Cosequ asked.

Rokura chuckled. "I'll explain soon."

CHAPTER 11. – MEI

A black mountain range obliterated half the starry sky behind Giloam's darkened walls, which had towered over Mei as she entered, but inside waited a bright, wakeful city of stone and glass and steel. Of spiced meat from cheerful street vendors in the markets, where men, women and children seemed only to laugh, smile and eat, scarves and tassels on their clothing fluttering as they moved about, and sometimes waved from the upper storeys of surrounding buildings.

From somewhere not too distant, the faint sound of drums and horns echoed – not a call to war, but music; and perhaps just as faint, voices singing. And at first, it was a pleasant, welcome sound among the din of voices.

Half the homes and inns seemed to be decorated in bunting, flags and flowers. Some people had woven glittering things within garlands that hung from their windows, while others had wrapped lanterns in coloured cloth of pink, green and yellow. She wondered how the cloth didn't burn, but such a detail didn't seem important, and the longer they travelled the cobblestone streets, the deeper Mei shrank into the wagon's seat.

So much colour, noise, and people. Everywhere she turned they filled the streets or buildings, crowded before inns, the swell of voices filling her mind until she clamped a hand over the bone earring... dampening the sounds, but it was not enough.

A weight had grown upon her chest. Her breathing was too shallow and she gripped the seat with a groan.

"Mei?"

She shaded her eyes with her hands. *I don't know what's wrong.*

"The inn I usually stay at isn't far. Can you hold on a little longer?"

I think I can.

"Where does it hurt?"

Mei shook her head as she fought the urge to gasp for air, pressure building in her temples. Mamalo quickened their pace as best he could. Even so, she was beginning to sweat when he stopped the wagon. He helped her down but her vision was somehow all too narrow, only her feet and the stones seemed clear; a line of green sandstone in the centre.

She focused on the coloured stone as she walked, giving occasional short answers to Mamalo's questions until she came to a halt – someone had opened a door. A new voice? The shape was blurred, but a bright blue seemed clear enough.

Once inside and seated upon something soft, a comparative quiet fell over Mei and she sat still, hands folded in her lap, breaths coming easier. Her sight began to clear too, even the pressure in her temples was fading.

"Mei, can you hear me?" Mamalo knelt before her, his dark, silver-flecked stubble now clear – though the blue was gone;

he still wore his usual black.

I can.

"This inn is run by a friend of mine, Iabe. I'm going to get some water and some food, all right? I won't be gone long."

Thank you.

Mei lay back upon the bed with her eyes closed. Now, she was able to draw air into her lungs steadily. Extra details drifted back to her awareness – muffled movements from another room, lowered voices, fainter ones from the crowds outside, and what might have been the clank of pots and pans from the inn's kitchen.

And none of it overwhelming.

"What *was* that?"

Villages like Cangola hadn't created the same effect. What was so different about the busy streets of Giloam? *I can't afford to let that happen again.* If Iggy was in a city somewhere, how could she search for him, let alone *rescue* him, if she couldn't stay in control?

And what if something similar happened to him?

Was Iggy in a city? She sighed. Was he even still within Nasaru? He had to stay near water... but how far could he have travelled, alone and probably scared? Her worry did not end there. *What if I've actually travelled* away *from him by following the river the wrong way? Or the wrong river?* "I really have to find a sorcerer."

The door creaked open, revealing Mamalo holding a tray with bread, fruit and water.

Mei took the tray and ate quickly. New flavours hid in the bread's crust and sweet stings from the fruit caused her mouth to water, even as she shovelled each mouthful in.

"Careful you don't inhale the tray too," Mamalo said as he glanced to the closed window where bright lights shone from the buildings opposite. "I didn't realise the Festival of Earthly Stars was tonight. I'd lost track of the days, to be honest."

Mei ignored his joke about her hunger, as curiosity took hold. *What is it about? Is it a long festival?*

"One night only," he replied. "It celebrates the repulsion of Senoja from the city, sometime last century, from memory. The date escapes me, but it is a happy day here. Earlier, there would have been a fire column of green and blue lit upon the western wall, symbolising the colours of the old duchy."

Mei took a long drink before asking another question, linking her thoughts to the words. "Does that mean I should stay inside tonight? Tomorrow too?"

He shook his head. "Resentment doesn't linger here, like in some places. At least, not so much that you'll experience outright hostility. Visitors and traders from Senoja are not uncommon in Giloam."

Is that who we'll be negotiating with first? Visiting traders? Mei shifted upon the bed. Not being able to speak or understand Senoja was definitely going to be a problem.

"No, I have someone specific in mind but I think we should start by finding a sorcerer – in the morning, of course," he added as he rose. "Well, if you need anything I'm in the next room."

Mei stood. *Oh. Isn't that... the expense?*

"Enjoy a proper bed. And don't be concerned about the cost. We'll make plenty more soon enough. Sleep well," he said as he left, closing the door behind him.

And you.

Mei returned to the bed, made from a similar wood as the walls it seemed, and stretched across it with a faint smile. *This is nice.* Her body settled into the soft mattress and Mei sighed. Her eye-lids were already quite heavy... and the unknowns and problems of tomorrow were distant and dim as sleep closed in.

***

The litter of coloured paper and leaves swirled around the streets, though the residents mostly seemed happy to sweep it up – save for the young ones, perhaps. They grumbled as they pushed their brooms around half-heartedly.

Thankfully, as Mamalo had predicted, she did not draw angry gazes. Few stared at all; people had their eyes on their meals or their work. Many ate as they walked, taking bites from meat upon sticks or between thin slices of bread, some even carried glasses and mugs – to return to inns and taverns?

"Here we are," Mamalo announced.

They stood before a pair of wooden buildings, supporting beams constructed in arches. There were even diamond-shaped frames within the windows... unusual, considering all the surrounding stone architecture.

Is this where a Coral Sorcerer lives?

Mamalo nodded as he climbed the short flight of steps and reached out to ring the bell, its round shape somehow cheerful, welcoming. The musical sound echoed across the street. "Sorcerer Onolse has an excellent reputation, especially outside the military – making him somewhat more affordable, though I cannot vouch for his services myself."

That sounds perfect. Not just in terms of a cost that she could not afford, but also in avoiding soldiers.

Mei exhaled softly as she waited, hopefully not so loud as

to catch Mamalo's attention. What would the sorcerer want in return for helping? *Could* they help? It was likely an enormous task, even for a powerful one. And how to explain everything? Iggy? She'd not even given Mamalo the full story; he knew she searched for her brother, that Iggy was powerful, but not the nature of his quest.

Or why we left.

There was even a chance that revealing too much would put Iggy in danger somehow.

Yet no other choice remained.

The door swung open to reveal a young man, a few years older than Mei herself, who smiled at them – a smile that she immediately wanted to see again. It was hard to look away; he was more than handsome too, almost beautiful where he stood in white and blue robes, an intricate design twisting and climbing up the sleeves.

Perhaps the pattern was meant to be like the mysterious Black Coral she was still yet to see, but the thought seemed to skim across the surface of her mind. Would his voice be just as compelling as his face?

"Sorcerer Onolse?" Mamalo inclined his head. "We would like to discuss hiring you, if you have the time?"

"Certainly," the man replied, and his voice *was* soothing, even after having spoken only one word. "Please, join me within."

Onolse stood back, gesturing for them to enter.

Mei followed Mamalo into a wide, open room lined with shelves and narrow windows at the rear. Beyond waited a garden path lined by purple flowers, leading around, perhaps to the second building. But Onolse took them to a pair of chairs before a long table. It, too, was filled with neat stacks of books and parchment and canisters in frames, with more of the same in a cabinet behind him.

The sorcerer took his own chair opposite and leant forward. "Now, how can The Great Onolse assist you both?"

CHAPTER 12. – MEI

The Coral Sorcerer regarded Mei for a long moment after she finished speaking, his dark eyes seeming to search her for answers beyond her request and careful explanation, and for some reason she flushed, glancing away.

Didn't I speak clearly enough? It had been a somewhat halting explanation, working through Mamalo, but the sorcerer seemed to understand. Why stare now? Didn't he believe her?

When she glanced back at Onolse, his expression had not eased; his interest in her story was very clear. Was he using magic? *If so, I can't feel it.* Finally, the sorcerer sat back, his handsome face now somewhat troubled. "You're not lying, of that much I am sure."

No, I am not, Mei said, speaking directly into his mind this time – some of her doubt gone at the suggestion she might have lied about her purpose. And while she *had* held back the truth about Nokema, she had explained, in brief, why Iggy left, and why he was both vulnerable *and* in danger from himself as much as others.

The sorcerer started. "Well…" His expression shifted from shock to interest to concern – the emotions fleeting but clear enough. "I do believe I can help you both, but I will need to undertake a little research. It won't take but a moment." He rose and moved to one of the shelves, his steps an odd mix of grace and forcefulness... or was it impatience? He tapped the spines of the books as he searched, soon bending to the bottom shelf with some grumbling.

"Ah-ha." He pulled a heavy, grey tome free and returned to the desk, beginning to flip pages, dust-motes rising. "The problem you face is that without having anything belonging to your brother with you, like blood, hair or fingernails and so forth, it is extraordinarily difficult to locate an individual in one nation, let alone across several, if that is the case."

"Then it's a question of more than the quantities of Black Coral," Mamalo said.

"Indeed, my good merchant." The sorcerer turned a few more pages, then slid the book around and pointed at a detailed image made up of long and short lines. A mirror with an ornate frame, carved to resemble eyes of all shapes and sizes. There were human and animal eyes; cats eyes, birds eyes and things that might not have been eyes at all, things that Mei could not fathom. And at the base of the frame, where glass met handle, a closed mouth.

"This is the Mirror of the Sky. Supposedly, it could be used to seek any and all, simply by chanting a name. *That* is the kind of power you would need for me to help you."

Does such a thing even exist?

The sorcerer shrugged. "Hard to say. But I show you this because I believe I might be able to create something similar, if lesser, with the right ingredients."

"But how?" Mamalo asked.

He chuckled. "Leave that up to The Great Onolse – it won't be easy, but if you can find a certain ingredient while I work on the rest, that would be most helpful. It would also enable me to offer you a considerable discount for my services."

"If it is additional Coral you need, I can have it shipped up the river and then across the foothills. It would take some time, of course," Mamalo offered.

Onolse shook his head. "Thank you, but while I *will* require more than I presently have on hand, there is something else in addition. Sand. Black Sand from the Raging Isle."

Is that all you need? She turned to Mamalo. *That doesn't seem so difficult?* Even if the 'Raging Isle' was not an encouraging name.

"Well, the island is not far from the harbour... but it's not a safe place," he replied. "I don't even know if we'll be able to convince anyone to take us there."

Why?

The sorcerer rested his chin in one hand, tapping a finger upon his cheek. "It varies, depending on who you speak to. Some say it is spectres of victims from an eruption in the dim past, others avoid the isle due to the sand-rippers, others due to the reefs or the jungle itself. Still others due to the curse. In any event, someone has succeeded in the past – since we sorcerers do know a little of the Black Sand."

Curse?

Mamalo cleared his throat. "All who have tried to bring back anything from the island have failed. Not so much as a jar of Black Sand or a piece of fruit. Not even a single leaf, supposedly."

Is that... then how could we ever succeed?

Onolse closed the book and rested his arms across the cover in a somewhat pensive gesture. "It is a significant risk, of course. But your task is urgent and I believe this to be the fastest course of action for me to make a lesser mirror. You could still try the military and its secrets... though that might pose its own risk," he said, then added something in what might have been the Senoja language, considering that she *mostly* understood it.

But she nodded as if she had fully comprehended his warning, then turned to Mamalo. *What do you think we should do?*

The merchant didn't answer at once, but when he did, it was with a sigh. "I think we should explore other options before the Isle."

From the corner of her eye, it seemed that Onolse shrugged but when she glanced at him, he was rising to return the book to the shelf.

Do we have other options?

"I don't know yet," Mamalo replied. "We could search every town for traces, either stories gleaned from residents, or by asking local sorcerers to seek far as each are able, but it would not be a swift method, obviously."

And offer little guarantee.

He nodded.

Onolse returned to the table. "You might also use your telepathy to try *reading* the minds of soldiers in each town to see if they are aware of a young man without a face... if such a thing is possible?"

Well, I'm not sure.

He waved a hand. "Merely an idea. In any event, should

you change your mind about the Raging Isle, I will certainly still assist you as best I can."

Mamalo thanked the sorcerer as he rose, and Mei followed him to the exit, where an older woman was entering. The sorcerer greeted his customer as Mei closed the door behind her, steps a little heavy on her way to join Mamalo on the street. What next? *I'm running out of ideas.* Coming all this way, meeting a Black Coral Sorcerer with a solution, only to fail now? Iggy could be anywhere. *How do I find him?*

"Don't give up, Mei." Mamalo started back along the street. "We'll think of something."

Thank you, Mei said as she kept pace, though it was hard to hold a lot of hope. *Where do we go now?*

"Well, my old friend Yalu has a business on the other side of the city. He might have some ideas, and I need to speak to him in any event."

About your trade deal?

"Yes. But it's not exactly a quiet part of Giloam, however. It's full of musicians – think you'll be able to handle that?"

Mei nodded. *I can.*

And more, she had to. Compared to last night, her breathing was normal, the pain in her temples gone. But even another Festival of Earthly Lights wouldn't stop her if it meant she could somehow find a way to Iggy.

She owed Mamalo too.

I just hope I can fool whoever we meet into thinking I'm Senoja.

CHAPTER 13. – MEI

Despite Mamalo's warning, his friend's workshop was no riot of sound.

Men and women in spotted aprons worked at long benches with clamps and littered tools, curls of wood-shavings everywhere; there were pots of varnish too, the sharp scent filling the space.

But no-one was shouting or crashing about with large hammers.

Many actually held small mallets and chisels, others using more delicate items she could not name, bent over their work with what seemed to be intense focus. They worked, spoke, smiled and laughed and sweated over tiny details like any other group of craftsman.

Aside from those entirely normal, even welcome sounds, there was the music of singing voices but again, nothing so riotous that Mei's mind was overwhelmed. Across from where she and Mamalo sat waiting in a smaller room with rounded walls of panelled wood, three men sang together. Each voice was a little higher than the last, blending almost as one. It was a wistful tune, but they were smiling – one even faltering at a mid-way point, and at the end, all laughed. Even Mamalo smiled.

That didn't seem like a happy song, exactly.

"They have changed the words. The true tale is of a soldier who must leave behind his beautiful homeland, his sincere doubts, details about what he will miss and so on, but in that version, the soldier left behind a wheel of cheese."

Before Mei could respond, a large man with wild, dark hair entered. He had a wide smile upon his face and his dark-green tunic with yellow tassels was open at the throat, showing the dark skin of his muscled chest. His boots clomped as he waved Mamalo down when the merchant rose, instead sitting beside Mamalo, slapping his friend on the back. "Alo, what brings you here?"

"Yalu." Mamalo smiled. "Business, I hope."

"Ah, too busy to visit your old friend simply for the pleasure of my company?" Yalu asked with a chuckle "What about this young lady from Senoja, then?"

"This is Mei," he replied. "She's going to help me negotiate."

"Ah, so that's what you've got in mind," he said. "I hope he's offered you a decent cut, young lady."

Mei nodded but did not speak at first. Would speaking into his mind be too much, without first warning him?

Yalu raised an eyebrow, though the question that followed was gentle enough. "A bit shy for a negotiator, aren't you?"

Mamalo leant over. "Go ahead, Mei. He can handle a little surprise."

Right. Pleased to meet you, Yalu.

The big man's mouth hung open a moment. "Did I just... I did, didn't I? You can speak with your mind?"

I can.

"And you can read minds too? Is that why Mamalo wants you to negotiate?"

Mei glanced to Mamalo. *We haven't really worked out the details, yet.*

The merchant sighed. "Forgive me, Mei. We ought to have done so, already. But my approach is simple enough. Senoja traders will only meet with nobles, or those few merchants already approved to trade. They do not meet with new clients. Our best chance is to surprise them as they return to the city of Kaarsi."

Surprise?

"On the road leading into the mountains."

Yalu tutted. "And that will clearly seem like an ambush, as I said before. How will you convince them to buy anything, even with Mei, when they will be returning after having purchased all their quotas?"

Mamalo grinned. "Obviously, Mei is my secret weapon but I do have something extra. Cresideth heart-leaf."

Yalu stood, as if unable to contain surprise – or was it excitement? "By Aehtu. How?"

"A tale for another time."

Mei glanced between them. *Just what was heart-leaf?*

Yalu took his seat again. "That I look forward to."

And what about me? How will I know what to say?

"I'll prepare you as we draw closer to the time, so expect to learn a lot about the heart-leaf. For the most part, you can simply translate what I say."

"Still a fair few days until they're due," Yalu said. "What will you do in the meantime?"

Mamalo gestured to Mei. "That is part of why we came today. Mei is looking for her brother, and so we're going to ask around. We'd appreciate any ideas you have for a head start around the gates, perhaps?"

"A few of the folk you'd remember from last visit should still be around." Yalu rubbed at his chin. "And to be honest, visitors from Senoja aren't unusual in the city. We're friendly with more than a few here, so I can ask around first, if you like?"

That would be wonderful... but I don't know if he's been this way. He... likes to stay near rivers.

Yalu put a hand on her shoulder. "Then I'll find Feeos. He works on the riverboats but I think he's in the city still. Maybe he'll know something."

Thank you!

"No promises, mind. He's a little short-tempered and, importantly, he's only one man. Might not have seen much at all."

"Sounds like it's worth a try," Mamalo said.

Yes.

"And you can ask around some of the obvious places too – west and north gates, Fisherman's Guild, even," Yalu added as he stood. "I'll check with the city-watch for you. Alone, of course – no need to bring down any unwanted attention. And I'll leave now since I have some errands to attend to anyway."

Yalu led them from his workshop and back into the streets, sending them north. He turned east, passing a row of stables and what might have been a fletcher, based on the customer that was counting arrows as he left.

It did not take so long to reach the gate, where Mamalo spoke with both the beggars and street vendors. Mei was silent at his side until he tried the gate guards, and then she remained some distance away. One fellow among half a dozen who sat around a gatehouse wore a different style of cloak, grey in colour, and he shook his head but pointed to one of the other soldiers.

A Greyshield, like Anyo?

A small voice spoke to her. "Excuse me, miss?"

Mei looked down to find a pair of children, a boy and a girl each holding little pink flowers. A flashing memory of Hisha and Hishi cut into her but she managed to smile. "Hello."

"Would you buy some flowers? They are sweeter than any honeycake."

Mei hesitated. If she spoke into their minds directly, would they be afraid? Or worse, report her to the guards? And after 'hello' and 'yes' and 'no', she would have already used most of her Nasaru words. And she'd not really used coins before either… how would she know how much to offer, assuming she had any to spare?

Before she could answer, Mamalo returned, wearing a slight frown. Upon his approach, the children strode off to chase a passing woman in orange and black silks, walking a skinny but graceful dog on a leash.

It hardly seemed worth asking Mamalo how his conversation went, based on his expression, but her question slipped free, nevertheless. *Anything?*

"No. Though I did not speak to each and every guard, I would hope your brother had at least made an impression on any who saw him. Word would have spread."

Only if he entered Giloam at all.

"Of course, but we're not out of ideas yet," he replied.

Yet the afternoon continued with the same list of failures, and with each one their weight grew. Mei found no spring to her step and even her shoulders had slumped; it ought not have been so disappointing. After all, she had allies and the ability to understand the language of a strange land now....

Almost mocking, her doubts lingered. *He might not have come this way at all.*

Mamalo gave her back a pat. "There's still Yalu's friend, remember?"

She nodded. Though Mamalo hadn't heard her last thought, her expression must have been gloomy enough. *You're right. Should we try to speak to him before nightfall?*

"I think so. How about we take a rest at the inn. I'll send a messenger and we'll see if Yalu can find Feeos."

Mei paused to focus on linking her voice to her telepathy, practising the deception once again. It would prove to be a very useful skill to hide her true identity when speaking with others. Like the much anticipated Feeos. "Thank you."

"Is that getting any easier?"

"It is." *But it would be easier if I didn't have to work to combine my thoughts and voice. Learning another language must be* extremely *difficult, if this is what it's like with all my advantages.*

He nodded. "It sure is. In my years trading with Cresideth, I've not learned nearly as much as I'd like."

Once they'd returned to the inn, sent a messenger and settled into the quiet of the common room, Mei found herself nursing her drink and nibbling at her plate of cheese and flat bread.

But Feeos arrived with Yalu sooner than expected.

The fisherman was a short, wiry fellow who limped over to

their table. Overall, his movements were sharp, something that became clear when he sat and snatched up the drink offered. He graced them with a pair of brisk nods, muttering into his greying beard, but did not curse or leave after hearing their query, something that had at first seemed entirely possible.

"Seen nothing like that. Been thinking it over since Yalu came to see me," he added, glancing to the musician. "He could have passed that information along himself, I might add."

"But you wanted a drink, right?"

Feeos nodded. "On your purse, I did."

"Well, did you see anyone unusual at all?" Mei asked, and while it *did* take less effort to cloak her telepathy the more she did so, it had her craving sunlight. "Even if you didn't see them clearly..."

Feeos seemed to be cleaning his teeth with his tongue, mouth closed while he considered her question. Finally, he shrugged. "Just a Greycloak, which isn't unheard of. She was sneaking around to the southern gate."

"Which leads to the mountains," Mamalo said. "Hmmm."

"You think that means something in particular?" Yalu asked.

"Hard to say. But whenever the nobility is involved in events, you know it's a sign of trouble – either underway or brewing."

"Will that be a problem for me?" Mei asked.

"Could be," Feeos said with a nod. "Or could just be that they're watching. Supposedly some duke is up to no good. Hiding tax revenue and the like."

"Best described as 'the usual', then," Yalu added.

The fisherman finished his drink and stood. He spoke a few words in the Senoja tongue, wishing her luck in her search, and after just a slight pause, she answered in kind – or at least, did so using Nokema words.

Feeos raised an eyebrow, even as he smiled. "I appreciate the formality of the old words, but I didn't help that much, girl."

"Sorry I haven't been able to help more," Yalu said as he too, stood. "But I'll keep thinking."

"I'll be in your debt, old friend," Mamalo replied.

"Also known as 'the usual'," the big man said with a grin as he left.

Mamalo chuckled as he joined them. "I'll compose some messages to some merchants I know and send them out. Someone might have seen him. We'll resume the search tomorrow."

Mei nodded but she raised one hand to the bone earring as she followed him from the common room. Could the magic help her understand more than one language?

It made sense that someone like Feeos who lived in a city not too far from the borderlands could speak Senoja... but for some reason, Feeos had understood her Nokema, calling it formal. And old. *But what I said was enough for him to understand. So maybe I'll be able to communicate with the Senoja merchants at least a little?*

If so, it was only one problem solved.

Iggy could still be anywhere.

CHAPTER 14. – MEI

The new morning was still young when Mamalo finished sending his letters, once again waving off her concern about the costs and of one day repaying him, of being in his debt.

Her promises were all beginning to seem a little paltry...

"I've been thinking," Mei said as they waited in the busy street. A pair of carriages passed, heading up toward one of the many peaked mansions with their black and blue tiles. The crest of the bear's head flew on all its flags. "There's still that sorcerer."

"The Great Onolse?"

"It was your first idea, after all. Should we try to get him his Black Sand?"

Mamalo exhaled long and loud. "It does seem like the fastest and most reliable method to find your brother, I agree on that front. But the danger... that island is a *bad* place. Always has been."

"This is a pleasant surprise," a new voice announced from the street behind them.

Onolse himself stood nearby, a pair of long-stemmed white roses in hand, his Coral-patterned robe bright beneath the morning sun. He smiled as he paid a girl nearby, who was carrying more flowers, then joined them on the corner – handing over a rose each. "I imagine you are both surprised also, but I am glad I found you."

"Found or tracked down?" Mamalo asked as he lifted the rose. "And what am I supposed to do with this?"

"Anything you please, of course," Onolse replied. "Think of it as a gesture of my request – I would like to hire you both."

Mei blinked over her own sweet-scented rose. "You? Hire us?"

The sorcerer nodded. "Yes. With my magic, your heritage, and Mamalo's wisdom, I believe we have a real chance of success at the Raging Isle."

Mamalo was frowning, his arms folded across his chest. "I think you'd better offer more than flowers, Onolse the Great."

Still the man only smiled. "Certainly. What did you have in mind?"

"An explanation," Mamalo said, and glanced across the street. Mei followed his gaze past the flow of people in their tasselled tunics, past tailors, toymakers and a shop that seemed to sell bread – rows and rows of bread of all shapes and sizes. So many shades of white, brown and even gold too... and when the scent reached her, she nearly took a step toward the building. Was Mamalo looking for a place to speak in private? It didn't seem the street would offer much.

"There," Mamalo said. "Behind the bakery. The coffee rooms."

"Coff-ee?" Mei asked.

Onolse chuckled. "You've never had coffee? It's something you drink. You'll love it."

"Then let's order some and you can talk," Mamalo said,

leading them across the street. His footfalls were sharp upon the stones, but he was pleasant with the smiling woman who led them through the bakery's interior. A corridor of mostly closed doors waited in the rear, some of which bore the hint of soft voices, but above each doorjamb rested a rune carved into the wood. The sense of power was faint, but it seeped from each doorway they passed.

Some sort of ward?

The woman paused before an unoccupied room, gesturing to chairs and a table set with cutlery and white porcelain cups – something she had only seen rarely, when Denuko visited. And for some reason, few in Nokema ever seemed to want such items.

There were no windows in the room, but vibrant plants with leaves tipped in red did add colour. "Shall I bring you anything?" their guide asked.

"Three coffees," the sorcerer said. "Mine with honey, please."

The woman paused, but Mamalo did not add any ingredients to his order.

And I have no idea of what I'm about to drink.

Mei sat and waited, filling the expectant silence with a few questions about the coffee, which was apparently made from crushed beans. It was also something of a delicacy. When the steaming cup was set before them and the door closed, a shiver fell across Mei's shoulders. She glanced around. Had something about the room changed? Because of the rune outside?

"Just the magic rune doing as intended. No-one can overhear us," Mamalo said, then pointed at the sorcerer. "And so I'd like that explanation now."

"No need to wave around such a tone. I meant exactly what I said. I want the Black Sand, and my best chance is to seek it with you. Once we return, I'll make a lesser Mirror of the Sky as promised, at no cost. After all, we're all taking on some risk here."

"We haven't set sail yet."

"True enough."

Mei noticed no-one had as yet taken a drink of the supposedly highly-desirable coffee. "Why do you want the Black Sand so much?"

"As I said, it is *extremely* valuable and useful. Like the Coral – only much harder to obtain, obviously. It will assist me with my future endeavours."

Mamalo leant forward. "That I believe, but I have another question. Why us specifically? There are other merchants, other folk from Senoja. Warriors, other sorcerers even. Why not form a grand force to undertake this foolhardy task?"

Onolse spread his hands. "I have thought to do exactly that, at various times. However, few would entertain such a quest. But I believe you are desperate enough to join me. Am I wrong?"

Mei didn't answer and Mamalo leant back in his chair.

The sorcerer shrugged. "It is no shame. I'm desperate too – as I said, this is likely my only chance to return with Black Sand. And get my revenge on that place."

Mamalo frowned. "Revenge?"

"Some years ago, the waves drove my master's boat upon the reefs. We barely survived, and of those that set forth, we were the only two to return." He gave a bitter laugh. "I never even set foot upon the damn island."

Mamalo lifted his cup and took a long drink from the coffee. "As inspiring as your story is, Sorcerer Onolse, there's a question you still haven't answered."

"Ask and you shall certainly receive."

"Why exactly do you think the three of us will succeed where others have failed?"

The sorcerer looked to Mei. "Because of this young Inora lady from Nokema village, of course."

CHAPTER 15. – ANYO

Chiotta rushed into the sitting room with a smile, crossing the space between herself and Anyo in something of a leap. He barely stood in time to catch her fleet form. "Chi?"

Her dark eyes were glistening with tears as she looked up at him – yet not from so far below as before; she'd grown taller over the last year. Her brown hair was still untamed and wonderful, and a single, slightly crooked tooth still threatened to undermine the maturity she'd gained with a cuteness.

But instead of her usual royal-red skirts, she now wore a pink tunic and her eye-make-up was in the curved Wisteria style.

"Why are... what?" His words came out jumbled.

"It's been a whole year already!" she said. "Have you been well? Why did you come back?" She held him at arm's-length a moment. "You're not hurt, are you?"

"No," he said, finally smiling in return. "I'm fine. And I'm back to continue my search, that is all. But what about you, Chiotta? Do you... live here now?"

"I do. At least, most of the time. Father thinks I'm working with House Tiger." She glanced at Lord Garakatka, who smiled back, the expression gentle.

Chiotta turned to greet Han and Katonga then. "Are you taking care of my foolish big brother, then?"

"Of course, My Lady," Han said after a moment's hesitation, he too, seeming shocked.

Katonga, on the other hand, only grinned. "I'll admit that he takes care of us too, Your Highness."

"That is what I had hoped to hear," she said, then turned back to Anyo, taking his hand. "So, you're here selling the family secrets for your quest, right?"

"I am. And you are... here? It seems a little treasonous, too." Somehow, if any of his brothers – and maybe even older sister Kiteka – had taken up residence with Wisteria or another house, it *might* have made more sense... but Chi? She was so sweet and loyal. *Wasn't she?* Even to the point of naivety... *Obviously,* I'm *the one who is naive.*

"Father was more than happy to share his tyranny amongst all his children, you know that, Anyo." Her cheer had faded a little.

"But..."

She raised her arm, finger extended. "If you've come to collect that dangerous Takirov woman and leave, then you don't need to know all of why I'm here. Just be happy you have the most extraordinary luck in all of history, since you chose the Wisteria tonight."

"She might have you there, lad," Han said from where he'd taken his seat again.

"I... very well. That is fair." Anyo managed not to add a caution that she take care of herself. She was no child, barely a year his junior in any event. If she was conspiring with House Wisteria on something, she had obviously made the difficult choices already. More, if she was working against Father, then all the better… and yet, was Garakatka the right man for her? "Then I will simply wish you success."

"And I for you, brother," she replied. "But before you leave, I think I'll need your help."

"With what, precisely?"

Lord Garakatka rose to join her. "Are you certain, Chiotta? I have already agreed to help him. For such a small favour, I need nothing more than what His Highness has already offered."

"I am," she replied. "Anyo, before you leave the city I want you to help me with a little distraction."

"From what? And how?"

"To your first query, I will keep that a secret as I know you're keen to vanish again. But for the how, all you need to do is… interview a particular man."

"Hmm. Go on."

"He is a sculptor working on Father's vanity project; I want to know more about what it's really for. Lately, his obsession with it seems worse."

Anyo frowned. The man's obsession had been in place for quite a long time. *Most of my life, really.* The enormous tree of Coral clearly was meant to be something more than a monument to his rule. "Very well, but why me?"

"Several reasons," she said with a grin. "You're leaving right after and if you do it instead of one of my people as I'd first planned, there's less chance of things being traced back to me. And it will upset Father when he learns you were here asking questions. That one's my favourite, to be honest."

He shook his head but he was smiling. "And this sculptor

is where? Can I also assume you've already paid him?"

She nodded. "Drinking at the Happy Tinker. It's not so far by carriage."

"Then we will discover what we can."

"That's why you're my favourite," Chiotta said, then led them from the room, Garakatka trailing with what might have been an expression of pride.

The lord arranged for a carriage with impressive swiftness, and then Anyo found himself seated in comfort, travelling along streets lit by the fanciful lamps of the city. Many were meant to represent flower arrangements, with varying sizes and shapes. It was, admittedly, beautiful.

What caught his eye was the graffiti, both carved and painted, most of it in Takirov.

Some in Nasaru, too, complaints about the king, usually.

Nothing new, then.

While they soon arrived, the Happy Tinker did not seem well-named from outside – a quiet place with soft lights and no music nor sounds of cheer from within. There was even a small carving of a grape-bunch with a line cutting through.

"Princess Chiotta said he'd be *drinking* here?" Han asked, doubt in his voice. Then he shrugged. "Either way, we don't have to do this, you know. Could be another big risk."

"It could be, but I find myself at least a little curious about Father's obsession," Anyo said as he led them inside.

The interior was not typical for the city's inns, either. It stretched down in a long, generous corridor lined with wooden stalls bearing no doors. Inside, people sat alone or in pairs only, served by young men and women wearing aprons and smiles.

It was a calm place, the clinking of cups or soft voices all that filled the space.

"Can I show you to a stall, gentlemen?" An older but not elderly man approached, pausing to lean upon his cane. "Kindly note, we serve a wide range of drinks but not ale, wine or spirits."

"I see," Anyo replied. "We are actually here to speak with Okalo."

"You will find him fourth from the end," the owner said. "I will send someone to take your order as soon as possible."

Anyo thanked the man and strode along as directed. He passed customers of a wide range of stations and professions on the way to stop before a slender fellow dressed in a patterned tunic, dusty boots extended beneath the table to rest upon the seat opposite. He glanced up from where he was examining a pair of silver rings, eyes widening… in recognition. "Yes?"

"Are you Okalo, the sculptor?" Anyo asked.

He nodded. "I am." He lowered his voice. "Your Highness."

Anyo exchanged a glance with Han and Katonga, both of whom moved along the room to sit or stand in separate positions, so as to monitor the Happy Tinker.

The sculptor moved his boots as Anyo sat. "I trust that I can rely upon your discretion here?"

"You can," the man replied.

"Wonderful. Now, I would ask you some questions about the Coral Tree."

Okalo hesitated. "I hope I can answer them."

"It has grown even more important to my father recently, hasn't it?"

"I believe it so. He doubled those of us working on it."

"And has he given you a deadline?"

"No."

Anyo lowered his voice. "Then tell me about the rumours."

"Your Highness?"

"We had our own in the palace over the years. What about amongst those working on the tree itself?"

"Well… there is something. It doesn't seem all that possible."

"Go on."

The sculptor slipped the silver rings into a pocket. "Master Ngame overheard some of the mages speaking. They believe the tree can be used to draw power up from the earth itself. Maybe enough to raze the entire city or more, if not properly controlled."

Anyo frowned. Was such a thing possible? And what exactly did Father want with such a vast amount of force? War and conquest? An obvious thing, but still one that seemed most likely. *Especially considering his speeches about the strength of our borders.* "The mages truly believe it possible?"

"At the very least, they fear it."

"I see." Anyo leant out, glancing from the stall. Neither Han nor Katonga were signalling that trouble was afoot, but it was likely time to leave already. *I hope this is enough for Chiotta, whatever she's up to.* He rose. "Thank you, Okalo. You have been helpful tonight."

"A pleasure, Your Highness." The sculptor rose himself, a hand half-raised. "If I could say one thing before you leave?"

"Yes?"

"I just wanted to tell you that I believe what you did back then was the right thing – to defend that Takirov, I mean. You showed real strength."

Anyo hesitated before thanking the man, and then he was gathering up Han and Katonga, heading from the unusual taproom in a slight haze of confusion. Not only because it was so rare to experience support for his past, but because of what he'd learnt. The Coral Tree was something deadly, indeed.

It really only makes sense if Father's goal is expansion.

And expansion meant war.

CHAPTER 16. – ANYO

After delivering the news to his sister, pulling her close in a long hug and biding her goodbye, Anyo found himself fleeing the city under the soft cloak of darkness once more.

Only this time, he was leaving while riding inside Lord Garakatka's rather lush carriage with its cushioned seats and, for whatever reason, fresh flowers. This time he was counting to himself as it rolled evenly through the paved streets too, with only the occasional bump or snort from the horses to disturb the passengers. *In any event, this is at least a more comfortable escape.*

Or it would have been, without Binya.

She sat beside him in her leather vest, bare arms revealing tattoos of graceful runes, some almost looking like flowers themselves. And while the dagger was not visible at her belt where she sat, her stare seemed a more than adequate substitute. There was something about the way her dark eyes burned. The bronze of her skin seemed almost aglow in the dim carriage too, as if she'd somehow stored light from the day.

Corpse-singer.

In decades past, Takirov corpse-singers—or Lirayx, as they

preferred—had been hunted and slaughtered by the Nasaru. Folk considered them Takirov demons, to be destroyed at worst and, at best, chased from each and every town or village. Doomed to roam the space between lands, between towns, between cities.

Slowly, things had changed.

Over generations, people came to fear the corpse-singers less, been less visibly eager to attack, less open about their desires to purge their communities of such 'filth'. And while many leaders preached tolerance, it left only a thin veneer of safety. Still, few trusted the Lirayx.

Binya herself bore a faint scar that ran down from behind her ear to her collar bone.

She had not volunteered the circumstances of her attack.

"While I am glad you have finally agreed to accept my help," she said, "I don't think sending brutes to drag me from my home was the smartest way to do so." Her accent was almost non-existent, considering how long she'd lived in the capital.

"Did they hurt you?" he asked.

Her scowl deepened. "I don't like being rushed. And I have commitments, some of which I am now unable to meet."

"I am sorry for that, but I'm forced to rely on less conventional methods while I avoid prying eyes."

"Such polite words, Your Highness. Can you offer me any assurances for the rest of our journey?"

Anyo frowned. "You agreed to come. In fact, you said you would not work for any other royal, and were the first to claim we would fail without you when last I set out." He controlled his voice but his frustration grew. "Obviously, you believe there is a chance we will succeed. That is all I can promise. You must hold your own against whatever we face, Lirayx."

She leant toward him, unperturbed by his words. "You don't have to worry about me in that regard."

"Good."

"Then it is time to seal our agreement."

He hesitated. "Here?"

Across the carriage, neither Han nor Katonga could conceal their frowns.

"You still don't understand, do you?"

"I do not, no," he replied. *Why would I?* Royals especially were prohibited from associating with corpse-singers, not that contact with *any* Takirov had ever been encouraged. *Though I certainly flouted that rule in a spectacular fashion, didn't I?* "I am aware of rumours and probably myths only."

"Is that why you doubted me before?" She shrugged. "Maybe it's not much of a surprise. I can't imagine a prince was given many chances to learn the truth about what we do."

"You have been offered generous payment."

"Which is only going to happen if you succeed. I need something more, as I have already told you."

He narrowed his eyes. "The 'soul-stealing' as they call it?"

"They? You mean your people?"

"I do."

Binya exhaled as she opened her hands, palms facing up. "You didn't even come across more accurate information as an exile?"

"My search was focused elsewhere. On other matters," he said, holding her gaze. "And is exploring the depths of my ignorance really a vital part of this agreement?"

"Just let me wallow a little longer in being right," she said with an evil-looking grin. "You dismissed me off-hand, and that was a mistake."

"Are you actually this childish?"

"Yes," she said without losing her grin. "But listen now, as I want you to understand. The rumours you've heard are no doubt full of inaccuracies and fears, but they come from a grave place. If you truly want my services, you must enter into this agreement willingly. If you do not wish to continue once you hear what I have to say, then stop this carriage and I will return home."

Anyo glanced down at her palms. "Am I supposed to take your hands?"

"Wait until you hear the rest. While I can most definitely sing to the dead, I may fail if the spirit is unwilling. More, I cannot guarantee I'll be able to learn what you need. The spirit is hardly guaranteed to share what you seek just because I ask. That is the risk for each and every song."

"That is not unreasonable."

"Good. Then I will ask that you pay my price now. Tonight, whether I succeed or fail later."

"Initial payment for your time and effort is not an outlandish concept," he said, yet took little comfort. Just what was she building toward?

"I appreciate that, Your Highness. So, we come at last to the price itself. Again, it is not the soul-stealing of which you have heard, but I will be taking something from you, Prince Anyo."

"That title is no longer mine, as you know," he said, and he used the words to counter a faint shiver of apprehension that passed through his body. "Tell me."

"I will take your secrets and your hidden desires; they will be mine," she said with a raised eyebrow. "Still interested?"

He hesitated. "What do you mean by that?"

"That there are some secrets you actually know you are keeping, and there are some you may not even be aware of, at present. Most people have secrets which are best described as things they have never even admitted to themselves, not once. They're stored deep within, only rarely coming close to their awareness. Sometimes, a person's secrets hide that way because if we ever came face-to-face with them, we would be disgusted. Or terrified. Or worse." She met his gaze. "For some who hire me, the curiosity becomes unbearable afterward. They demand to know what I have learned, and that knowledge can sometimes destroy a person. Anyo, I will know *all* your secrets if you agree, even those you may not be aware of yet. Do you still seek my help?"

All my secrets? Shameful things from childhood, like when I cast one of my brother's paintings into a well? Transgressions committed as a lovesick fool? *No, she's talking about worse things.* The carriage seat suddenly became uncomfortable, tension sneaking through his limbs. Baring all such secrets was one thing, but the Takirov woman was right – far worse, surely, was the idea that something was hidden within, deep enough that he didn't even have the courage to face it himself. That someone else would come to know such dark truths, could that be accepted? "I... do not know how to answer."

Han leant forward. "It is not too late to refuse her, lad."

Binya did not respond to his words, she only waited.

Anyo nodded. "I know, Han."

His mentor's expression was near to a scowl now. "You hold secrets shared, remember."

"I have never broken a confidence," Binya said. "My livelihood depends on it."

Still Anyo could not answer.

She met his gaze now. "It is a long ride to the Marsh and there are only two answers to give. Either you will take the risk, or you won't."

"Is this so different to blackmail?"

"Not all Lirayx are honourable, I admit. But I cannot judge those who use anything they must in order to survive. After all, what's to stop some Nasaru lord or merchant from taking us for our skills then refusing to pay once they have learned what they seek?" Her expression grew dark. "Or worse again."

Anyo shook his head. "This is almost more terrible than the rumours. And aren't you putting yourselves in more danger by doing this? After all, if you learn the secrets of the wrong person, you will become a target."

She shrugged. "I am always in danger."

He slumped back in the seat, as if her answer had sucked the tension from his frame. Or maybe it was simply defeat.

Binya *was* the only one who could help, despite his own doubts or Han's misgivings. But that was not all. Failure had stung, all the worse for coming so close to his goal. *I will pay her price. I will find the Sothalic and I will restore honour to my family, to my nation. And to my own name. Even if it means usurping you, Father.* "I will agree to your terms," he eventually said as he leant forward and took her hands. "My secrets are yours."

CHAPTER 17. – MEI

Mei straightened in her chair. *How did he know?*

Mamalo was glancing between them, cup half-raised. "Those hidden people?"

"Not precisely hidden. But among those who remember the Inora, few visit. And they very, *very* rarely leave their valley," Onolse added. "Of course, I should let Mei expand if she so wishes."

Mei's cheeks grew flushed. "Mamalo, I'm sorry. I... I let you assume I was Senoja."

"Well..." He lowered his cup with a sigh. "We all have secrets, I suppose. But to be honest, nothing has really changed. You can still help in negotiations, with your telepathy. And considering that your people fled Senoja long ago, the languages come from the same place, it might even be a little easier than you expect."

"I hope so."

He smiled. "At the very least, that will catch their attention. And if you can find a way to read their minds too, then I still have all the advantages."

Relief washed over Mei; Mamalo was taking her deception

quite well. As Onolse claimed, perhaps he was desperate to convince the Senoja to trade with him.

"Of course she will catch their attention. And no doubt your heart-leaf will manage the rest," Onolse added.

"You guessed?"

"Not that difficult, since you have one of the things Senoja crave most, but which they are prohibited from trading for – openly. And with Duke Bedoa currently being watched by the Greyshields, he will not be able to offload his own precious cargo. This is your perfect opportunity."

"Possibly."

"I admit, I'm most curious about *how* you managed this, Mamalo. Your timing is either extremely fortuitous... or you have other hidden skills?"

Mei reached for her cup of coffee, just for something to hold, since she found herself lost in a wash of words. The duke was trading in heart-leaf, it seemed. How had Mamalo obtained his own stash? And was Onolse angered? *Is this new alliance falling apart?* It was too difficult to guess. The names, places, implied relationships and secrets between them all. What did it mean?

"What's happening?" Mei asked. "I don't understand any of this. Mamalo?"

He took another sip of his drink. "I have unwittingly drawn you into something, but I reiterate my promise that I will help you find your brother."

Onolse leant forward. "I do enjoy secrets."

"Before that, I think some context will help," Mamalo said with a frown directed at the sorcerer. "For some months now, the king has placed Duke Bedoa under watch. The Greyshields believe he is involved in clandestine deals with Senoja – selling heart-leaf, among other things."

"And why is that a problem for the king? Does he suspect spies?" Mei asked.

"Doubtless," the merchant replied. "But there is another reason, being that Senoja sun-killers sometimes use heart-leaf to aid their dark arts."

"Oh."

Onolse waved a hand. "Mostly they use it for pleasure or sell it on to Viareya at an inflated price."

"Either way, if one of King Mutolo's vassals is involved, as the Greyshields think likely, it will reflect *very* poorly on the king."

"Reputation is everything."

Mei finally lifted the cup and before it reached her lips the rich scent had her mouth watering… and then the first taste was like a bitter poison. *I hope this stuff didn't cost a lot of money.* "That all makes sense, I suppose," she said, doing her best to control any hint of distaste upon her features. "But what does that mean for you, Mamalo? Aren't you selling the heart-leaf to the Senoja? Won't the Greyshields come for you as well?"

"Perhaps not if he's *also* a Greyshield, my dear," Onolse replied. "It would also explain how a merchant knew precisely when to bring such cargo through Giloam, at a place and during a time when its duke lay so close to ruin."

"So it would appear." Mamalo leant back in his chair. "But you're not quite correct."

Then you're not a Greyshield? Not a noble? Mei slipped back into mind-speak.

"Former on both counts," he said with what seemed to be a

sad smile, though the expression did not linger. "But Sorcerer Onolse has the truth when it comes to my knowledge. Meeting Mei was a stroke of fortune but I have not lost contact with all of my former comrades. Duke Bedoa and his lackeys skirt very close to ruin indeed, and I do mean to take advantage of his greed."

"And the same greed is not your own?" the sorcerer asked.

"I dally with no spies."

"Just contraband?"

Mamalo's voice grew hard. "Just contraband."

Once again, there was a sense that more tension lurked beneath the obvious ones between the two men, but she had her own questions – for the sorcerer. "Why are you so convinced I will make an important difference at the isle?"

"It is my belief that you will be able to communicate with the spirits that may remain."

"With my telepathy?"

He nodded. "As The Great Onolse, I am certain."

"And if you're wrong?" Mamalo asked.

"That does not happen very often."

Mamalo grunted. Mei frowned at the sorcerer; it was not just his words that were making him appear somehow less handsome. Was it the bravado? Yet, far more importantly, was his claim actually one of truth? Or some ploy to ensure she and Mamalo risked their lives at the so-called Raging Isle to win him his Black Sand?

"Mei, even if he's right... the Isle is too great a risk," the merchant said.

Onolse raised a hand. "Before you decide, I want you to answer honestly – isn't there something I could create for *you* with the Black Sand?"

"Plenty of things," Mamalo replied with a shrug.

"Then you would benefit also."

"Too risky."

The sorcerer sighed. "I do have one final card up my sleeve. One more to join our expedition. Someone I believe will be just as useful, even without Inora magic."

Mamalo shook his head.

Onolse chuckled as he stood, then moved to the door – opening it to reveal a young woman whose dark eyes were as bright as her smile. Her hair, just as dark, bore tight curls and seemed almost alive. She wore a cloak of grey tied at the throat, concealing whatever weapons or other items she might carry.

She took a seat at the small table. "Have you agreed yet, Alo?"

"Nata." Mamalo returned her smile, though it did not fully reach his eyes, making it more an expression of wariness. "Why are you here?"

"In Giloam? I think that's obvious."

"In this coffee-house. With this sorcerer."

She leant across the table, reaching out to rest one hand upon his shoulder. "You know the answer to that also. Everyone who ever left the ranks always said how hard it was to untangle themselves from the Thread, Mamalo. If you help the kingdom once more, I promise not to mention your little infringement in my report."

Mamalo answered from behind clenched teeth. "How very kind of you."

CHAPTER 18. – ROKURA

The feeling of being watched lingered during the next day on the road out of Oris. Rokura informed Cosequ and Iggy but even with three pairs of eyes – or two and one mind – at work, the watcher was not to be found within the stony fields or between the gnarled trees.

These bore the same dark scales from the mountains but there were more ghost-gums too, with white bark and brush-like blossoms of yellow that drifted down on the spring breeze.

Takirov bore its own beauty, hard but with touches of delicacy; a fact easy to miss beneath the tension of bloody bitterness.

And up ahead, the cause of it all.

But that isn't precisely true, either.

The lead wagon of a modest merchant-caravan had overturned, spilling Black Coral onto the paved road. The huge heap spread across the route in jagged, uneven clumps that blocked passage at least partially. Equally, bodies being dragged into the ditch were a far more grim an obstacle.

And a tragedy that could have been avoided.

Nor was it merely two or three lives lost, but at least a dozen.

Most of the dead were bandits in mismatched gear, though

it seemed many had painted the same symbol of a fist upon their clothing. The rest of the fallen were Nasaru soldiers sent along to guard the Coral, their red tabards matching those worn by the men and women who worked to clear the road. The bandits were tossed into the dust, swung by their arms and legs, but the stricken soldiers were being arranged carefully on the opposite side of the road, arms at their sides, weapons too.

One is still alive. Iggy pointed toward a spot some distance from the attack, to a small stand of pale trees. No movement within.

"My Lord, please help us!"

A merchant waved to them. Blood covered his hands, his sleeves and his collar where he knelt beside one of the fallen soldiers, tears trailing down wrinkled cheeks.

Rokura nodded to Cosequ, who was already reaching for a vial of Black Coral as he leapt from his mount.

"I'll return," Rokura said as he dismounted. "You might be safer with me, Iggy, just keep your hood raised." He drew his knives as he threaded his way through depressions and piles of stone, some of it twisted Coral so leeched of colour and magic that it was no longer even grey, but now a powdery white.

Spots of blood, and sometimes splashes of it, led to the trees Iggy had pointed out, and when Rokura pushed between the branches, he found the survivor.

A young Takirov, his dark eyes wide with pain as he gasped for breath. His ragged tunic was covered in blood from several deep wounds in his torso, obliterating the clumsily-painted symbol of a fist. Crimson smeared his face too, trickling down from a cut upon his forehead. A small axe lay by his twitching hand.

"Nasaru... pig."

Rokura sheathed his blades. Just how much older was the young saboteur than Iggy? Barely two or three years. And he had thrown his life away for what? "Why did you do this?"

"What?" The lad was blinking hard.

"Die for a few wagonloads of Black Coral?"

His eyes blazed. "Because... it is... not... yours!"

What does he mean?

The bandit grew still. Rokura sighed, then started back toward the wagons. He spoke over his shoulder. "He was talking about the Coral."

Which is heading to Nasaru for your sorcerers.

"So, you do understand."

What I meant was, does he think that merchant stole his Coral? Or cheated him and his friends somehow?

Rokura paused. "No. He means that all Black Coral should belong to Takirov, and that when my ancestors invaded and took control, that they were wrong. And that today, I am a pig for being born in Nasaru."

So, the Nasaru just take all the Black Coral from the Takirov? There seemed to be judgement in the voice that was very clear in Rokura's mind.

"Not without compensation."

...Less than they would receive if they sold it to your sorcerers themselves.

"Yes," Rokura said. "But that isn't all. We build hospitals and roads, defend the south from Senoja attacks or attempts to steal the Coral. Our sorcerers heal Takirov without prejudice – even after years of attacks like this."

And that's enough?

"Enough what?"

In exchange for total control of such a powerful thing.

Rokura exhaled. "There's a long history."

I see.

Yet from the tilt of his head, it did not seem that Iggy understood. "We'd better see if the merchant needs help."

Iggy followed in silence.

At the wagons, some relief was visible in the badly-wounded guard, who now sat up against one of the wagon's wheels, suggesting Cosequ had saved the woman. The old merchant stood off to one side, still breathing hard.

Other survivors – handlers, more merchants and guards alike – were reloading the wagons, and lifting one back to an upright position with a roar of effort. It thumped down with a crack.

"Stay with the horses," Rokura told Iggy as he joined them. He bent to collect the Coral, using his cloak as a hamper. The Coral was so dark as to swallow the very light, hard as stone beneath his touch but there was a warmth deep within; the pulse of magic.

Of power.

He glanced to the stand of trees as he dumped the Coral back into the wagon. Was it worth such bloodshed? By his second load, the other corpses had drawn his eye too. Had any of them deserved such a death?

The merchant approached. His eyes were still red-rimmed, but he reached out to take Rokura's hands. "Thank you, My Lord."

"I have done little. It is Commander Cosequ who has completed the true work, here."

"And I am in his debt also," the merchant replied. He glanced back to where Cosequ attended to guards bearing other injuries, helping one fellow into a sling. "Was the mountain pass clear?"

"It was," Rokura said.

The older man sighed. "That's a relief to hear. Thank you again," he said, returning to his wagon, a limp slowing him.

"We ought to leave ourselves," Rokura said when Cosequ finished, and together they returned to Iggy and the mounts.

This time, Rokura led their tiny group, moving beyond the wagons at a trot and farther along the road, speaking little, save to postpone a meal. And why not, considering his appetite had vanished.

Eventually, Iggy's voice echoed in Rokura's mind. *How far to Atanoph?*

Rokura glanced around for a road-marker but found none. Still, it shouldn't be too hard to guess. "Two or three days from here, I'd estimate. Cousin?"

Cosequ nodded in agreement.

Will we face an attack in that time?

"Perhaps, given the isolation. We will post a watch each evening to be certain."

"Will you sense any danger with your mind?" Cosequ asked Iggy.

The lad turned to face the surroundings and Rokura studied him. Just what did the young fellow see? Iggy had tried to explain a little more, but the description of his sight remained vague. It seemed he could not perceive colour. He did say that he had no trouble recognising people or places, objects… but that certain other things were beyond him.

He also added that in some ways, he saw more than others.

I should know, whether human or animal, if any approach — but unless their intent is clear, I don't know if I will be alerted while sleeping.

"I doubt any rebels will be able to hide their intent," Cosequ replied. "Their treacherous thoughts will scream forth, I suspect."

Rokura tapped Arrow's flanks. "Then let's find an agreeable campsite before night falls. I'd rather not be ambushed on the road."

That, I believe, I will at least sense.

CHAPTER 19. – ROKURA

Despite the spectre of attack, no bandits, rebels nor traitor struck of an evening, nor while they rode the broad highway the next morning, a mild sun beaming down upon Rokura's face.

In fact, even with scattered homes and fields of the thin blue-stalk found within the hills leading to Atanoph, they passed no travellers and saw few farmers harvesting or tending to the hardy rock-sheep of the south. Certainly, no-one approached or spoke to them. The Takirov Rokura saw all focused on their work.

Not until the pale stone walls of Atanoph did Rokura converse with a stranger – spending little effort convincing weary Nasaru guards with their slumped posture that it would be no trouble at all to let them in, not for a Greyshield, a sorcerer, and their quiet charge.

But while Cosequ enquired after the duke, Rokura stared up at the walls – as he did every visit to Atanoph. Battle scars had not been covered, and only a few times repaired with darker stone. For the most part, the gouges spoke of boulders and catapults, of rams and Coral Gnashers, but it was the towering statues set in deep alcoves that captured his gaze.

That, and the memories they brought.

From the open palms and raised arms of the warrior Minav clothed in Takirov robes and woven circlet, there had once hung a message of peace – for a short time only.

The clumsily-painted plea was soon torn down, of course, and once more the city fathers began to debate destroying all such Takirov symbols… and in doing so, set off yet another round of riots, where smoke, fire and blood had filled the streets.

If Oyo were still alive, would she despair that so little had changed? Would anything ever change? Violence always led to violence, she would have reminded him, sadness in her husky voice.

The myth of progress.

Inside the city, the prickly sensation of being watched fell over Rokura once more, but he ignored it for the time being.

Here, like in most southern towns, an unwavering, narrow line of stone in the street offered directions to important buildings – healers, money changers or accommodation, mostly. In Atanoph, the stone was a far darker colour where it ran through an open market. Bright stalls lined the buildings, their arched windows lit by the sun. Most were several storeys tall, some with Takirov beads hanging before the doors and others with Nasaru crests.

Lines of rope ran between many buildings, most with little buckets attached, so that neighbours could pass food or other items between.

But no window contained an observer Rokura could see.

Whoever watched was no novice. *So, when do I flush them out?*

"Want to ask around about the Sneaks before we resupply?"

Cosequ nodded as they passed a pair of fruit sellers, both with scowling Takirov owners; one of them even went so far as to cover a small bowl of strawberries as Rokura passed.

At the very next stall, this man was of Nasaru origin, and Rokura noted an equally untrusting fellow, considering his glare coupled with folded arms. *My cloak.* Not all considered the Greyshields – or any noble for that matter – worthy of respect.

What are Sneaks? As before, Iggy walked between the horses, head down, face-covering half-concealed by his hood. *Is that a person... or, an animal perhaps?*

"No. It's just a term to describe how the merchants and stallholders here hide their messages about who they will take care of."

Take care of? You mean they will charge you less for some reason?

"Yes. For some, they will not even sell to you if you aren't Takirov. For others, no service unless you hail from Nasaru."

Is that really the case?

Rokura nodded. "It is. We'll ask at an inn, or the local Quiet House and see what is current." At the Quiet House at least, he knew the leader well.

I'm not sure I'm putting everything together. What exactly is 'current', and how does it relate to the Sneaks?

"Well, the merchants change the signals regularly since the city tries to stop the practice – so we'll ask about that. More importantly, we can seek Brutan and the duke's movements at the same time. He may not have come through here at all."

I'm sorry, Rokura. I'm still not sure I understand the Sneaks. How would anyone know? How does the city stop this practice?

"While we walk," Rokura said, leading his mount toward a wide thoroughfare, this one lined mostly by taverns and smaller, speciality shops. These boasted cheap food and money-hatches or lavish window displays lined with queues of people waiting to purchase Takirov delicacies like the honeycakes.

Compared to his youth, few owners at such stalls seemed to be Takirov.

Rokura?

"Yes. As I was saying, the so-called Sneak is usually a symbol hidden within the price or description of an item, or sometimes something pinned to a wall or the counter. As a customer, if you see and recognise it, you know to shop there because you will pay less or be given better cuts of meat, as an example. It was a trident symbol at Nasaru stalls one year, as I remember."

I see now. So people share the symbol to help each other avoid being taken advantage of, but the city tries to stop the entire process?

He nodded, though Iggy probably wasn't able to tell. "Once a symbol is known widely enough, the city begins to issue public notices. Sometimes they fine or even close stalls that continue to use them. And so the merchants change the Sneak and the game starts over again."

Iggy still kept his head lowered as he walked, but it seemed as though he had nearly turned a few times. *I understand what you mean now, but... I still don't know why. Is it because of all the tension I feel in this place? To me, it feels like no-one trusts anyone else here.*

"Perhaps an exaggeration, but not so far off either," Cosequ said, his voice soft.

"And that's a far more complicated question," Rokura added. "One we don't have time for now. We need to plan our next move."

"What does the disc say?"

"Ever southward," Rokura replied.

I need to find that clue to the location of the Mistress.

"Yes," Rokura said, and though Iggy turned to him, he did not add anything more. The lad's plan was still folly, nothing had changed there, but if it came down to attempting to force the Iggy to stay or chasing after Asaro Itonye, then Iggy would have to come second to the royal bastard.

CHAPTER 20. – ANYO

Though Anyo knew the way, the trip through the Malkaha Marsh lasted longer this time, longer than the wandering and trial-and-error of wrong turns and shifting islands, of searching for insects, or even detours to capture possible sun-killers.

This time, each step was heavier. Each moment of respite, shorter. And no matter if the moment was simply to take a drink from his flask or something more substantial, like sleeping within his tent of a night, he achieved no true rest. His dreams were always unsettled, and in the long hours of daylight, Binya was always watching.

Even when she was not at all close.

Even when she was focused on her own tasks or asleep herself – even when he crouched by her tent to listen, to be certain that the regular breathing from within could only suggest the pattern of sleep... the corpse-singer was watching.

She knew *everything*.

And more... even what he did not know himself, *she* knew.

Sometimes, he shuddered when she approached. Merely to discuss directions, the tomb or the legend of the sword, to help around the camp with the cooking or foraging… And for all the time his skin crawled at being watched, at being exposed, *he* watched *her*, waiting for a sign that she would expose him, that one of the truths about his quest for the Sothalic would be revealed, disappointing Han and Katonga, or something worse.

Or that she would make her first move toward extortion.

… and the days and nights passed as they neared their destination and it never came.

Is she waiting to strike at a time I am most vulnerable?

Almost more confusing; she was not living up to the worst of what he expected – or what he had been taught to expect. Just as often, Anyo had to leave the camp to lash out at some undeserving sapling or hunk of muddy earth with a makeshift club, or to hurl stones far into the swamp, their pitiful splashes hardly enough to satisfy his foul temperament.

Anyo knew, despite an inability to admit it whenever Han or Katonga asked about his dark mood, that whenever he slipped away from the campsite, that he was lashing out at himself for letting temptation dig its claws into his mind.

What else did she discover?

At best, whatever secrets Binya knew were not enough for her to abandon the quest, nor turn away in disgust whenever she saw him. That, or she was a fine actress.

Usually, after he had finished destroying whatever undeserving lump of vegetation had borne the brunt of his anger, he would return to the camp and speak not a word of it; attend to some minor task or discuss the path ahead, then seek his rest – though such a word was generous.

And when they eventually drew near Rinbe's valley, just as

evening started to settle across the marsh, bringing a cool dark with it, after he had left to once more vent his anger and finally stopped to catch his breath, footfalls approached from behind.

He turned with a sigh.

Binya.

She glanced at the wreckage he had wrought but did not mention it, only regarding him with an intense gaze, something that seemed both perpetually filled with anger and perhaps even curiosity. But strangely enough, she offered no judgement – not for the whole trip so far, and not even now as he stood before her, gnarled branch in hand and chest heaving.

"What do you need?" he asked, his words short.

"Nothing."

"Then why are you here?"

"Because there is a question you refuse to ask me," she said. "In truth, you have held out far longer than most and I admit to being impressed. But if you are not careful, it will devour you."

He tossed the stick into the dark water. It vanished with a soft splash. "Concerned?"

"For my employer?" She smiled now. "A little. After all, you must succeed in order to compensate me."

"I will not ask you anything."

"No?" She moved closer, standing before him now, frown on her face. "As I have already explained, I will share nothing that I have learned with another – only with you, should you ask."

Anyo clenched his jaw. *What* did the woman know? But he did not – or could not – speak, despite the urge to move his tongue, to discover what darkness lurked within him, to learn whether he could face down his hidden self.

"For some, it brings peace. They no longer have anything to hide, even from themselves. They come to know themselves far better. Such knowledge can be a great boon, if used properly."

"How many ask?"

"I have sung under contract for fifteen people only. All but two had me reveal their deepest secrets after the terms were fulfilled." She gestured to her scar, hard to discern in the fading light. "For one especially, the answers were not to her satisfaction."

A reminder that Binya, too, took a risk by entering into the Contract. "And those who resisted?"

"I have not seen nor heard from either since. They could have gone mad or lived happy lives for all I know."

He exhaled. "This isn't offering me peace of mind."

"I was not exaggerating before. Plenty of people have found a powerful peace."

Anyo glanced back to the murky water. "I do have something to ask."

"Of course."

"Of the fifteen times you have worked under contract, how many spirits refused you?"

Once more, Binya smiled; perhaps a hint of surprise in her eyes now, as if she had expected a different question. "None."

"Then I look forward to sharing another success with you on the morrow, Lirayx."

She inclined her head and turned to leave. "I will strive to meet the obligations of our arrangement."

Anyo watched her walk away, another question on his lips

– about the fates of those who did *not* take satisfaction upon learning their own deepest secrets – but he did not open his mouth, instead letting her return to the warm glow of the camp.

Eventually, he followed.

CHAPTER 21. – ANYO

Rinbe's home had remained undisturbed. Black and green hints of poison stained the kitchen walls and floor, but below, beyond the shadowy passage in the shrine itself, no suggestion that Marhyn had returned to attempt further treachery.

It would have been quite the unwelcome turn of events if either the sorcerer or the toad-creature appeared. Perhaps especially true of the slimier of the two – and still Anyo wondered, had the man survived the marsh? If so, to where had he vanished?

The Sothalic was more important.

Anyo almost smiled as, once more, he found himself crowded into the shrine with Han and Katonga and joined by another foreign woman, someone he hoped could win him his answers.

Binya brushed at the stone before the tomb as she knelt, then bowed her head. "This will be no soothing song, gentlemen, but do not be alarmed."

"Right," Anyo said, though he did not understand. *So long as she can prove that the blade is inside. Or find out where it lies.* "Do you recall the questions?"

"I do."

She began to speak softly then – to herself or to the dead – but as her voice was a low murmur, he could not guess at the words. Were they Nasaru, Takirov or something else? There was an ethereal quality, with an insistent tone too.

He glanced to the carven coffin, to Rinbe's bearded features. Nothing seemed unusual; no voice answering from within, no rumbling or grinding, not even the suggestion of movement. Nothing came to darken their lamps either, no sudden sweeping chill... just Binya's voice.

"Hark!"

Anyo flinched.

Binya had thrown her head back, shouting to the dark ceiling of stone. She called again, louder, and her chant resumed too. It was set to the same rhythm, but now words no longer sprung forth. These were *sounds*, becoming increasingly forceful, her voice growing raspier, even seeming to tear as she screamed.

He took a step back.

Was it a scream of pain? It continued, just as rhythmic as before. He exchanged glances with Han and Katonga, both of whom appeared equally taken aback. Binya continued to scream her 'song', though if such sounds bore any melody or words now, both were too enigmatic to fathom.

From within the coffin, *something* seemed to glow. Faint light of a deep blue was barely discernible, as if passing outward through the very stone.

A chill swept over Anyo – of anticipation.

On Binya screamed, torso tensed, muscles in her neck straining. Her voice grew more ragged but still she did not stop, though the pace of her cries had slowed somewhat. Did she need a little more time between screams?

Was she not in pain *now? Surely!* He hesitated before creeping closer, but her arm shot out toward him, hand raised.

And still she screamed.

"This cannot be right," Han said, raising his voice.

Binya fell silent before Anyo could answer. She slumped forward again, head bowed, but she waved them closer, using both arms now.

Anyo knelt beside her.

When she spoke, her voice was a bare whisper. "Brin sent the Sothalic away with his wife and child before his death. Mishaina was travelling to Senoja. To a place that was special to them both."

Anyo gripped her by the shoulders, disappointment mixed with excitement. "Binya, where? What was the special place?"

"He… did not say." She lifted her head. Up close, tears of exhaustion filled her eyes and flecks of blood were visible upon her tongue. "There is one more thing… to share. But let me rest first."

The end of her sentence was so faint that he was not certain he heard correctly, but he nodded. "Here, lay on this," he said as he rose to remove a bedroll from his pack, helping her lie down, where she closed her eyes, still breathing hard.

Katonga was already bringing water, which she rose to sip from before smiling at him and settling down again, closing her eyes once more.

Anyo motioned them into the passage, keeping his voice low. "Well?"

Katonga shrugged, and by his somewhat blank stare, he

could have still been hearing Binya's screaming. "I had heard rumours, but that was…"

"Kat, not Binya."

"Yes. Well, there was more than one story about Rinbe and Misha sneaking west, wasn't there?"

"Assuming we believe her." Han rubbed at his throat as he stared back into the shrine.

"You heard what I heard, Han," Anyo said.

"True enough."

Anyo nodded. "Then we're going to follow this new lead."

"Senoja is a big place. Not all that friendly for us either."

"Which is why we need to think," Anyo said. "What could a place that is special to both of them be?"

The older man gestured. "*This* seems to be the best bet for a meaningful place."

"Then there must be a clue," Anyo replied. "In something we've either read or heard. Some hint in one of the stories or legends. We didn't chase down all those books for nothing, right?"

Katonga grinned. "There was the account of the Wandering Scholars, stolen from Lord Sabo's library, yes? We fed his guard dogs all that meat and it actually kept them quiet until Han was handing it out. One bit his hand, remember?"

"I do remember that," Anyo said with a smile of his own.

Han seemed less impressed. "One of those books mentioned that Misha was said to be a fine singer. It is a small detail, but I wonder."

"What do you have in mind, Han?"

"Some link to Senoja there?" Katonga asked.

"Perhaps. The was another historian… Finalu, she said

something about Misha... called her a 'radiant songbird', I think it was." He scratched at his white beard. "For that detail to be recorded, perhaps she was a *very* fine singer."

"Ah." Katonga nodded. "You're thinking they travelled to have her take the Twin Trials at the Guild of Bards."

"Could be."

Anyo rubbed at his neck. It was a lead, at least. "All the way to Liialle?"

"Probably a slim hope," Han admitted. "It's more likely they would travel to see *family* – perhaps distant relatives in this case. Obviously, I don't know how we would even begin to try that theory."

"I agree," Anyo said. "But we found rumours of them passing through the villages in the west, and Kaarsi too. It was a trading centre even back then. There's a chance they did leave the marsh more than once; I always thought that possible."

"So why not Liialle too?"

"Right."

"We could follow, seeking local histories as we go," Katonga suggested. "We'd be heading west either way."

Anyo slumped against the nearest wall. "Yes, but in the end, it's probably just not enough, is it?"

"I think we're missing something obvious," Han said, and pointed to Binya.

Anyo glanced to the Lirayx, who was breathing evenly now, her eyes still closed, hands folded upon her chest. Han was right, but there was a problem. "We don't know where Misha is buried, if that's who you want to ask."

"Close. I was thinking any one of Rinbe's descendants."

Katonga slapped a hand against his own thigh. "The Senoja

silk scandal."

"What is that?" Anyo asked. When it came to the royals, the word 'scandal' was hardly a unique descriptor. *Except for Grandfather, at least.*

"This is certainly before your father's time, but there were reports of a young commander of unclear heritage who wanted to marry a Senoja noble. Supposedly, the lad was denied by the king of the day on account of his Nasaru blood. Now, that's not unheard of by itself, neither here nor there, but the gossip that eventually reached the palace claimed he had tried to offer *royal* Nasaru blood as a measure of his worthiness."

"Why haven't we come across this story before?" Anyo asked. "And why is it referred to as a 'silk' scandal? I would have thought I'd have heard of it, with a name like that."

"Well, it is one of several similar fanciful tales collected across the years following the wars. Now, it might not stand out amongst all such rumours, save for being one of the more recent I'm aware of. I'd hope it would be easier to chase down; that's why."

"It could well be," Anyo replied, and the task seemed to stretch before him as a new, even more insurmountable obstacle of old names, old secrets and yet more distant places. "And the silk?"

"Supposedly, the commander hung himself by silks taken from his mother's wardrobe – from the parapets of Giloam, near the border."

"Oh." He sighed. "Whether we follow the path of the songstress or seek a possible descendant, or both, we must obviously travel west."

"And take the corpse-singer with us," Han added.

"Think she'll be willing?" Katonga asked.

"She has fulfilled her part of the bargain but I will offer her more. Whatever is left of my fortune, if I must."

"Will that be enough? She may not want to risk her life further, and in an unfamiliar land."

"If Binya refuses, I will have no choice but to come up with an alternative," Anyo replied with a frown. What *would* she demand in order to continue helping? What was left to ask for? *She already has my secrets. She could ask for anything and I would probably agree...*

"If you say so, lad."

CHAPTER 22. – THORN

Upon a small hillside, the Coral Tree was nearing completion. Its woven branches spread in a dark canopy that nevertheless let fantastical shapes of light stream through and splash upon the paved ground.

Soon, Ibila, soon. Thorn let himself smile as he watched the sorcerers, masons and sculptors at work. Most toiled to construct branches upon long benches, affixing Coral pieces to one another via thin spears of melted Coral. Their practised movements became hypnotic as they slid piece after piece of the hard Coral onto the spikes, which entered as if driven into clay.

After which, the branches would be added to the tree – the largest ones to the trunk, but at such a late stage of the process, most new branches were being affixed to the canopy via ladders and scaffolding, again with sorcerers keeping careful watch and using their power to keep the tree together.

At other points, masons sanded away to create smooth streams upon the trunk at four points. Apprentices in their smocks worked with pan and brush to collect the valuable dust that fell to the stone.

Upon Thorn's arrival, one of the sculptors approached with a wide grin. Ngame, known for his animal creations of marble, and master of the school that Thorn had basically employed to complete the Coral Tree. "Your Majesty, it is wonderful that you have chosen to visit us."

"And this is wonderful progress."

"Everyone is working to their full capacity," Ngame replied. Then he hesitated a moment, before remarking upon the weather.

Thorn did not address the pleasantry. "You have a question, do you not?"

"Yes, My Lord. I wonder, as I have for some time now, if it wouldn't be better to open up some of the canopy for aesthetic balance, you see –"

"I can only imagine there is some suffering when a patron prefers what they wish to see over what a master knows is best, but that is my wish, as well you know." And while there was a very fine reason indeed, the sculptor could hardly be given the truth.

Despite the monstrous potential for power the Coral Tree represented, it might still fail as part of a cage – not to mention, as a constricting death-sentence for the Moon Father. *At least, with help from the siblings.*

One of whom could soon be found near Kaarsi. *Which must be my next destination.*

"You are generous to humour me, Sire."

"A great artist deserves at least as much – and more, should you still wish to create something of your own vision for the palace ballroom."

The man straightened. "Most assuredly."

He smiled. "Then I will leave you to finish the Tree. Within the month."

"It will be so."

Thorn strode off, heading back toward the brightness of the palace.

Once inside, he took the quieter halls and passages reserved for servants, finally reaching his quarters with an impatient snap to his footfalls. He gave the guards a bare acknowledgement as he pushed the double doors open, breaking the Wing emblem to enter the spacious reception area.

Long ago, he had replaced the various war paintings with works that depicted more striking mixes of animals: the proud peacocks, noble stallions, a golden lioness and also one image depicting small, red and black beetles resting upon bright leaves, dew drops like diamonds between them.

Ibila approached from an adjoining room, following his gaze as she joined him. "I've never quite liked that one."

"The way light has been painted is quite something, I always thought," he replied with a smile, drawing her to him and cupping her cheek with his hand. "Though we have more important things to discuss, I am sure."

She met his gaze, her dark eyes holding the expectation of disappointment, it seemed. "Such as how long you will be away while you retrieve the sister?"

"That is not the first order of business, but yes."

"Then you had better have something important for me to do while you are gone, Mutolo. I am not willing to be 'kept', as I'm sure you know."

"Not my intention."

She stepped away but took hold of his hand to lead him

from the reception area. "Then tell me more, someplace we won't be overheard."

CHAPTER 23. – ROKURA

"And that is all you can tell me?" Rokura asked Waroja.

He and the Warden of the Quiet House stood upon the balcony, staring across a darkened garden with its blue-black leaves soft beneath light from decorative lamps, each one carved to closely resemble a hand holding lantern.

Waroja nodded, the silvery hair of his long plait swinging slightly. "It is. No sign of Duke Bedoa or anyone on the road that might have been smuggling prisoners. There is the usual unrest in the city, but nothing that should concern you as you pass through."

Rokura sighed. "I see. I thought there'd have been some sign at least."

"None," the man said as he rubbed at his clean-shaven chin. "But there was one thing – an odd report."

"How so?"

"Admittedly, this seems impossible to verify, but it didn't strike me as the work of rebels or discontents at that. Chosa found a message written in strange, bright-blue paint. Seemingly not comprised from anything we recognised either. It mentioned the 'Moon King's return'. Nothing at all like the

Takirov commonly write."

The Greyshield Warden was right. Such a thing did not seem usual for the Takirov, nor did it seem connected to Brutan or the duke... *Quite unlikely. But there is an old adage about the incurious being afforded no chance to complain about surprises.* "Something caused you to recall it just now."

"Perhaps. Still, I doubt it is of concern for your task. We will be watching for more such messages."

"No ideas on who this Moon King might be?"

"None. Though it likely means nothing," Waroja replied. "It was found on the side of a merchant's home – a woman in good standing. It was at least a week ago now; I ended up dismissing it in the end."

"I see." The more Waroja explained, the less likely it seemed to be related to Brutan and the missing prince. Rokura pushed himself from the rail. "I appreciate your time, Warden. I'll seek my rest now. And thank you for bending the rules this night."

"Of course, old friend. Just make sure none take note of your young charge."

"I will." But when Rokura returned inside to descend the nearby staircase, he found himself heading for the exit.

Restless or impatient? The watcher still needed to be flushed out. Perhaps it was time to attempt exactly that.

The streetlamps were spread few and far between but he strode along the stones, making no effort to conceal his movements, though nor did he stride about as if to draw attention. If the watcher had followed him to the Quiet House, they would become aware of his leaving soon enough.

And though the hour was not so late as to make the streets empty, the sound of following footsteps soon reached him.

The watcher paused when he did, followed when he turned into quieter streets behind the fire-lit market, and only when Rokura stopped to examine the sign upon a lamppost did he hear the footfalls behind him come to a halt once more.

He spun and charged back the way he came.

A figure in a dark cloak stiffened, then fled down a narrow alleyway.

Rokura did not slow. Down several other side streets, once flashing past the bright windows of a music parlour, and then into the darkened back streets again, the figure now running harder – drawing away.

The watcher leapt around a broken fountain and slipped down another alley but Rokura had not lost his target; he followed, keeping the slapping footsteps as a guide, and when he slid into a garden plot with fragrant shrubs, he stopped.

Two figures struggled over an open lamp – a Nasaru merchant, his collar askew, hair wild, and a younger Takirov man in vest and pants. They stood over a pile of paper bark creations scattered from a wicker basket, the intricate detail clear even in the shifting light. Some of the creations were entire castles, while others of animals like the lion with a magnificent mane, or a pair of figures dancing in coat and gown – the famous Takirov art, delicate and beautiful and sealed in a thin resin mixture…

… and highly flammable.

"What are you doing?" Rokura ground out the words.

The merchant lashed out with an elbow, knocking the Takirov to the ground. He stomped on one of the artworks and held the lamp over the pile – his guilt plain for any that might see.

The man only sneered when he noticed Rokura. "I can't see how this concerns you, Greyshield."

"You don't?"

"No." The merchant spat. "It's just the work of some little Takirov pig, who cares?"

Rokura took a step forward. "Have you even a shred of honour?"

The merchant laughed. "You think I care about that? This is survival, fool. And you might be a lord, but you're nothing compared to the Guild. My word is their word."

He pointed to the artwork. The Takirov man seemed dazed where he lay groaning. "Destroying the livelihood of another person like that is not survival."

"Oh, but it is, Greyshield. Because life *is* a competition. But you would hardly understand that – especially born as you were with every advantage, yes?"

Rokura narrowed his eyes. "If you cannot succeed as a merchant without resorting to sabotage, then your problems clearly have nothing to do with my life. Cast the lamp aside – I warn you now, but once."

"Or what, Greyshield?"

Rokura drew a blade. "You are horribly mistaken if you believe the Guild is the higher authority here."

The merchant sneered, though he was blinking hard now – an odd combination of expressions. Drunk? The scent of alcohol was not so strong that it reached across the distance between them. "What are you, then? Some sort of pig-lover?"

Rokura clenched his jaw. "Extinguish that flame now."

"No." The man's arm was trembling. "And there's nothing you can do to stop me; why can't you understand that? *No-one* will care about some mud-eater's trash." He dropped the torch.

The flame hit the artwork and bright orange bloomed.

Rokura threw his knife.

Steel flashed between them to thud into the man's leg. The wretched fool stumbled back, face twisted in shock, and Rokura was already leaping after – fist crashing into the merchant's face.

The man collapsed with a grunt but Rokura ignored him. Instead, he bent to snatch at some of the bigger pieces of art, but the blaze was already out of control – fire snarling as dark, acrid smoke rose, forcing him back. Cries of despair echoed from nearby. The artist. The fellow had reached his knees, blood pouring from a reddened eye-socket.

Rokura turned on the merchant instead – who was dragging himself to his feet with incoherent muttering – and kicked the man back to the cold ground.

The fellow grunted again. Rokura leant in and tore his blade free, blood splattering across the stones, eliciting another cry of pain. "By the Authority granted me by King Mutolo, I will now execute you. What is your name, merchant?"

The drunk's eyes widened in pure terror. He clutched at his bleeding leg, cringing into the stone. "No! I'm important!"

"Then die nameless in my record," Rokura replied.

Rokura plunged his knife into the man's chest.

The merchant stiffened. Blood spread from the steel, creeping across the man's tunic and he screeched no more.

Rokura heaved a sigh as he removed the knife and rested the bloody blade at the foot of the corpse. Then he removed two more knives from his belt and boot, and stood waiting. He glanced over to the trembling artist. Rokura gestured to the fellow, whose face was also streaked with tears. "Come quickly, please."

"I… My Lord…" The fellow rose and approached, glancing between Rokura and the corpse and the still-burning remnants of his work. His hands were clenching and unclenching.

Rokura unhooked his purse and handed it over. "Go to the city guard, anyone in a red cloak, truly, and send them here. Keep the money."

"I… I don't understand." The man wiped at his eyes, wincing as he did. He was younger than Rokura first assumed and the coins clinked where he held the purse in trembling hands. "You… killed him."

"Go now," Rokura repeated with a gentle nod.

"But…"

"All is as it should be; there is an order to everything that follows."

Still the Takirov artist hesitated. "I-I should thank you… but even that… I, my work."

Rokura offered a smile, though it probably granted little comfort. "Forgive my failure."

Fresh tears welled in his eyes and he turned to run from the small garden.

Rokura waited. It was easy to consider his actions justified, but he had let his fury get the better of him. Would the resulting Hearing cause a delay? Still, even if the Guild did choose to get involved, the merchant had wronged. Their word was hardly law.

No, but mine is – a responsibility I have likely abused this night.

And the watcher had escaped too.

Equally troubling, was the thought that just maybe, the

watcher had led him to the garden? Unlikely, surely.

When a trio of city guard finally appeared, Rokura remained in place, making no movements that might be considered threatening – not due to concern, but process and conduct was everything after killing in the King's Name. "My name is Rokura of House Rose, Lord and Greyshield. Send for others to clean and collect the body, along with my blade. You must also send someone to the Quiet House. Inform Lord Waroja that Lord Rokura has Executed an as-yet nameless merchant."

"At once, My Lord," the more senior guard replied after glancing at the scene. He sent one of his fellows off ahead, leaving a single man behind, as he in turn set off in another direction.

While the remaining guard obviously knew enough about the Greyshield codes, he kept his hand near his hilt.

"Worry not," Rokura said. "The Code guides me. I will not leave this place until Lord Waroja arrives."

The guard nodded but did not reply.

Rokura stretched his arms and torso as he continued to wait but did not – and could not – take a single step from the Execution site. All that remained now was to be escorted to the lord's chambers, and there, to convince those who would be convened to compensate the Takirov artist.

CHAPTER 24. – ROKURA

Rokura rose when the heavy bolts slid free from his cell door, letting daylight into the windowless room with its single bed and bucket. The light revealed Cosequ and Lord Waroja, both wearing grim expressions. *Waroja isn't acting as Justice? What does that mean?*

"It is time," Waroja said, stern expression revealing nothing, which, in and of itself, was a sign.

Something is amiss. "Of course." Rokura joined both men in the chill of the hallway, the Quiet House living up to its name. "Is Iggy safe?"

"For now," Cosequ said. "I thought it wise to keep him out of sight. Especially considering –"

"Observe the Code, Lord Cosequ," Waroja said. "This is to be done in silence, now."

Rokura followed them into a wide chamber decorated by the shields and blades of previous Lord Commanders, smaller crests of the noble houses set in the windows.

Three figures were seated at a stone table. A long tablecloth of white covered the surface, its symbol of linked hands – the symbol of the Justice – near to touching the tiled floor. While two of the Greyshields wore cloaks and gloves, the woman with greying hair in the centre wore no gloves but instead, a purple mask that covered only the top half of her face, with holes cut for her eyes.

Had tradition permitted Rokura to approach much closer, the stitched symbols of the blade-like leaves would also have been clear on the mask. Even staying put, twelve paces from the table, even masked, the identity of the Justice was clear.

First Daughter, Princess Kiteka.

Why?

She was in Atanoph for negotiations... but why had she taken it upon herself to become involved with a Judgement? She had every right to act as Justice, but in the past, she had only cared about the glory of the king, about suppression of rebels...

Is this a reason to worry? I have *followed the Code.*

Only twice before in his decades as a Greyshield had Rokura performed Executions, under somewhat different circumstances. And then, he had plenty of witnesses and supporters. Yet today, not a single Voice had been called. None for the Executed, and none for the Executor. *They have prevented the Takirov merchant from speaking. And the family and associates of the Nasaru.*

The princess spoke, her voice dispassionate but bearing a trace of impatience at the formality, since they were both known to each other. "You are Lord Rokura of House Rose, Greyshield of Nasaru."

"I am, Justice."

To Waroja and Cosequ, she nodded. "You are released from your duty here."

Waroja stumbled on his reply. "Y-yes, Justice."

Cosequ hesitated, but Waroja had already turned to walk from the room. Yet the sorcerer still offered Rokura a nod before following, his own footfalls heavy in the hush of the room.

The princess waited until the door closed, glancing down to whatever she held before her.

"Justice." Rokura lowered himself to one knee. "This appears unusual. Why do you break from the Code in this gravest of moments?"

The woman did not lift her eyes. "So it is."

Rokura waited. Exactly what was afoot?

The merchant... The fool hadn't been talking himself up? He actually possessed friends in the Guild powerful enough to influence the royal family? Surely not.

Even if so, it did not matter.

The Code was sacrosanct. Even – especially – for a princess, someone who relied upon the Greyshields as irreplaceable vassals.

Yet doubt had already wormed its way into his mind. *Are you forgetting the Beggar Prince? He did the right thing, and look what it earned him. Royalty doesn't automatically equate to honour – even a child knows that. You* know *that.*

Finally, Princess Kiteka lifted her gaze. "Your name is to be Struck from the Register."

At first the words did not register.

Struck?

Rokura shot to his feet. "Your Highness!"

"I am only a Justice in this room, Lord Rokura."

"Justice." He took a step forward, and somehow, his voice remained steady. "I have acted according to the Code."

"I agree." The woman did not continue, she only stared

across the table. Neither of the Witnesses spoke, their gloved hands, used to object, utterly motionless.

"Then I ask that I be allowed to bear a different consequence."

"That is not an option."

Rokura clenched his jaw. It didn't make sense! None of it – least of all his punishment. Why? Unless… Was the whole process actually an all-too-obvious trap? If so, devised by whom? And last night, where had the watcher disappeared to?

Who was the watcher?

A fury was building within him, tightening his very chest with a chill that somehow sucked the power from his voice – he did not shout; his words were calm and cold. "And why is there no other option, Justice?" Rokura could not keep a sneer from the title.

The woman rose slowly. "Your tone is questionable, Lord Rokura."

"As is your judgement, Your Highness."

A dread silence followed his words.

One of the Witnesses beside the princess twitched. Kiteka's hands curled into fists upon the table… and then she lowered herself back to her seat. "You are to hand over your cloak and crest. Both will be burned, according to the Code. You can no longer act as nor for the King, nor use His Majesty's pigeons nor benefit from his largess, nor expect privilege in respect to inns, nor take comfort in the Quiet Houses. In recognition of your years of service, you will be permitted to reside within Nasaru, but know that any infractions against King, Shield, merchant or citizen will earn swift retaliation."

There was more to the speech but Rokura was already removing his cloak. He let it fall to the floor then reached into his empty purse to tear the rose crest free, and this he tossed after – all while the princess was still speaking.

"Your land and any assets will be sold to the Crown. A percentage of proceeds will be held at the palace so that you may start a new life, yet you may not use any of that money to act against the nation in any manner whatsoever, upon pain of death."

Rokura turned and strode for the door, as the 'Justice' continued to read her stinging words, words he had last witnessed as a Greyshield-in-training, and proclaimed for the traitor Varnom, whose murderous rampage ended an entire House.

As Rokura reached for the handle, the recitation stopped.

"Lord Rokura, wait."

He paused but did not turn.

"In spite of what must be done, I have dispensation to offer –"

"I do not care."

"Imbecile!" Princess Kiteka's voice echoed in the largely empty room. "You would throw away your life for some Takirov worm?"

Rokura turned, jabbing his finger at the woman. "The Code is for all, or it is for no-one! Surely the First Princess of the realm understands that much."

"I see." Kiteka folded her arms. "Then you needn't concern yourself with the Code, now that you no longer wear the grey."

"I hardly need a piece of cloth to act with honour," Rokura snarled as he left the room.

CHAPTER 25. – CINDER

The men introduced themselves over the hiss of shovel-blades sliding into dirt. Paragon Mikal, the elder of the two; and Galarik, who did not seem as welcoming. While both villagers worked on the graves with stoic expressions, three bodies resting beneath blankets nearby, their watchfulness did not fade as they explained their warning.

"An old evil walks the valley. Mostly at night," Mikal said. And again, while his accent was strong, his vocabulary was certainly broad enough. "We call them *arkedi*. In Nasaru, it might be translated as 'stalking sand', perhaps."

"Worse than the extremely large cat-beasts littering the village?"

"Yes," Galarik replied, his accent much heavier.

"The *arkedi* appear as gleaming sand and while not swift like the Blood Cats, they can take on shapes that ensnare whomever they approach." Mikal paused his work. "Even in death, they are dangerous."

"How so?" Cinder asked with a slight frown. With no evidence of such things, it would have been easy enough to believe the so-called Blood Cats had been responsible for the empty village, but on the other hand, what reason did the Inora have to lie to a stranger?

"Each grain can cause illness and death, or searing burns at best. Unfortunately, it is quite impossible to predict how each person will react," the man replied with a sigh. "If you choose to join us in the caverns, you will see."

"A nearby refuge?"

Mikal nodded as he resumed his work. "Pass through the village and take the trail leading up into the hills. Do not tarry and heed the markings, for some grains still linger."

Cinder thanked them with a nod and strode back toward Nokema. This time, he skirted the homes, easily finding the trail.

The path lacked paved stone but wasn't fully overgrown, and he soon reached a fork. One side led higher into the wooded hills. The other, toward something of a plateau with a dark opening; the cavern entrance was half-covered by purple ivy where it overlooked the village and bright wheat fields.

And leading to the refuge were the markings he'd been warned about.

Stakes, really. Littered along the earthen trail, sometimes within it also, wooden stakes were arranged in half-circles, or sometimes standing in pairs or alone. All cut in haste, they'd been driven into the ground hard enough to splinter the wood.

As promised, they indicated the presence of so-called grains.

Cinder knelt before one, keeping his hands to himself for a change – there was a heavy sense of unease, a scent of ash. And citrus? Whatever the case, the bright grain of sand seemed to be burning in place without exactly charring the dirt. Nor fading.

"Best you do not touch, my friend."

Cinder blinked at the speaker. A merchant approached in his dark clothing and numbered collar, hat in hand as he scratched at his head.

"Fine advice," Cinder replied as he stood.

"You are far from home…?"

"Cinder. And I am indeed, not unlike yourself, good merchant." He regarded the man. Was the pleasant fellow only a merchant? Or Greyshield in disguise? Hardly an unheard of occurrence. Especially of late, while bickering at the border was said to be simmering hotter than it had in decades.

"Denuko," the man said with a small smile. "Regrettably, you have come at a time of strife."

"Mikal and Galarik explained."

"I see. It is worse to witness, but if you take shelter and assist us here, the people of Nokema will protect you."

"That sounds fair." Only so long as necessary, however. The city waited, where a certain dagger needed selling. "Though I do wonder how I might help, being a simple traveller."

"There is plenty of work for willing hands – and a simple traveller would have little trouble gathering herbs or even heating water, I'm sure," the merchant replied, gesturing for Cinder to follow.

Cinder did so with a nod, passing more barriers that marked leftover grains of luminous sand.

Or, pieces of the *arkedi*, the sand-stalkers.

"Even without the sand creatures they mentioned, this village has suffered much, from what little I've seen."

Denuko glanced over his shoulder. "It is all quite connected."

"Is it?" He detoured another half circle of stakes, this more like a fence that extended deeper into the space beside the cavern's opening. "How do you mean?"

"The Blood Cats have been driven from their lairs in the south by the *arkedi*," Denuko replied. "There is a great fissure being investigated. For now, it impedes passage south."

"Then would I need to head back the way I came to reach Omaila?"

"Possibly." Denuko paused then. "Speaking of which, I am curious. How did you make it through the Moon Gate unscathed?"

"You mean the passage beneath the mountain?"

"Yes. The village believes it to be the original source of the sand-stalkers."

"I saw no such threat," Cinder said with a small shrug.

"Hmmm. I do not know if that is troubling or not," the merchant replied as they reached the cavern entrance. The refuge bore no defences, but more men in green robes and dark pants stood watch. Both carried short bows, but something about the air within the entryway suggested an undercurrent of other defences. More evidence of the so-called 'mind powers' of the Inora?

Despite receiving looks of suspicion, Cinder was admitted to an impressively large cavern where he found what must have been most of the village; some two score people, perhaps. They were working on various tasks, some separated by makeshift curtains and others in groups.

One woman was brushing the hair of a child, and while the girl swung her legs as if enjoying the attention, her gaze did not seem focused on much of anything at all... almost vacant. Most conversations were hushed and the adults spent a lot of time watching the cavern-mouth.

The village's refuge was also spacious enough to house what was obviously Denuko's wagon, where the merchant fed Cinder a modest meal of fruit, nuts and some cold meat. All of it delicious, considering his hunger.

No-one approached, but as soon as Cinder finished eating, Denuko was leading him to the rear of the cavern where another somewhat smaller room waited. Here, people moved between makeshift beds with water or medicine, patients resting upon piles of leaves and blankets.

"Some cannot be woken," Denuko explained.

Such victims were very still, expressions calm where they lay. They *did* appear to be breathing, but most wore bandages with glowing spots beneath the wrappings, a tint of blue to the light. Unnatural enough, but worse was when one stricken man opened his mouth – not to speak, but for gleaming silver drool to escape.

"The village healer, Arun, is doing all he can to discover a cure but has made little progress."

Cinder shuddered at such a fate. The threat of the sand-stalkers was growing more visceral.

Raised voices echoed from beyond.

In the main cavern, Mikal had returned, a frown upon his careworn face.

Others gathered around as he explained… something. Cinder looked to Denuko, who soon translated, speaking softly. "Ketaj is returning with news, but his message was unclear… They are considering sending someone to check."

Agreement may have followed, then the conversation seemed to shift.

"What now?" Cinder asked.

Again, Denuko listened for a time. "Basically, Mikal and the other paragons are continuing a conversation they have been having since the attack. No-one can agree as to the reason why the *arkedi* were able to strike without at least *someone* sensing something sooner."

Cinder nodded, then waited. The discussion had not grown animated precisely, but frustration and even desperation was creeping into the voices.

And then the entire cavern fell silent.

Cinder looked from face to face. What had happened? It was as though the Inora had all felt something troubling at precisely the same moment.

Mikal straightened, jaw clenched as he made an announcement.

Denuko's translation followed on the heels of the paragon's words. "There is a column of *arkedi* headed for the village."

CHAPTER 26. – ANYO

The lands west of the Malkaha had a barren aspect; greying earth, cracked stone and spreading across it all, strands of dark moss… but it was not a dead place.

Little insects with sturdy bodies, and snapping lizards were plentiful. The farther they rode across the plains, the more signs of civilisation they encountered – mostly fences in states of disrepair.

At an abandoned farmstead, two walls only remained of its home; and wind pushed dust across the empty fields where once, some manner of crop must have flourished.

Anyo walked with a hand upon his hilt despite the lack of people or complete buildings, for the road carried an expectant feeling. As though something were going to happen, or someone return. Like a faint hum? Once, when they had stopped to eat travel-rations at noon, he examined some weeds and their purple flowers, finding them swarming with dark blue wasps, their segmented bodies and clear wings making a hum.

At the time, he had backed away slowly, warning the others as he returned to their small circle.

"Are they really that dangerous?" Binya asked.

"Yes. The poison could kill any one of us within a day," he replied. "Westerners use their honey for medicine, however."

"I don't think I've ever heard of them before, you know. And I didn't think wasps made honey."

"These do."

Katonga glanced back to the patch of flower. "We're lucky blue wasps aren't that aggressive, to be honest."

Binya seemed to give him a closer look. "You're from the west?"

"I am." He shrugged. "But that was a long time ago now. Nor do I carry a whole host of happy memories about the place."

"Ah."

And they'd moved on, travelling along the same road until it became paved, expanding to a width suitable for wagons by the third day. Over time, the amount of wasps had dwindled but according to Katonga, most would be within hives owned by farmers. Such people were rarely seen themselves – even as their surroundings changed to a fairer mix of green and gold grasslands.

Not long after another simple meal of travel-rations on the fourth day, Anyo brought them to a halt at an intersecting crossroad. One branch led north toward the River Kobade and eventually, the ocean. Turning south meant landing in wilds of Takirov, but it was the path farther west they had to follow. Beyond, the enormous mountain ranges of Senoja waited, not yet even a haze upon the distant horizon.

Katonga pointed to a smaller trail and a stone marker. "The village of Minyor is down there. We could stop for more supplies before heading on to Dibora. There, we might be able to find some clues and hopefully some horses – it's a little larger, if nothing else."

"Good," Anyo said. From that point, each step toward Senoja would be significantly swifter.

Somehow, doubts that had started to weigh more heavily upon him in Rinbe's home were easing… perhaps even Binya's eyes bothered him a little less now too. Because she had agreed to continue helping? *At no small cost, of course. And she still knows all of my secrets. That has not changed.* The Takirov woman had not agreed immediately, pointing out the danger and yet more time away from her other commitments.

"I promise you more again, more than what I have already pledged," he had said in the cool of the tomb. "Once I have the sword, I can change Omaila – I will take my father's throne and make it safer for your people. Heal the rift between our nations."

Her eyebrow had raised. "Bold claims, Beggar Prince."

"But I make them with sincerity."

"So I believe – and have in the past. Very well, I will help you," she said, already having to whisper once more due to the pain in her throat. Not long after recovering, she explained some of the difficulty in winning Rinbe's shade over, but promised she would be more than ready to sing to whoever was needed.

"What was he like?" Anyo asked.

"Gruff, but kind. He only agreed to answer when I described some of your more noble secrets – and so you had better live up to his expectations."

Anyo had only been able to nod in response at that, awe, doubt and pride jumbled within him.

And now, as they approached the walled village of Minyor in the dusk, and passed through its tall wooden gates to search for lodgings – an Indifferent House, if possible – Anyo could have fooled himself into thinking that *Han* now held all his secrets, and was especially displeased about what he'd learned.

After all, the old timer's glare was heavy enough.

Even Katonga appeared at least somewhat bemused as they led their horses along a wide, dust-choked street. Few buildings in Minyor were fully constructed of stone, those that had second storeys were made of timber but more noteworthy seemed to be the torches and braziers, burning a deep orange. The braziers shaped as birds with blazing wings were a fine lip-service to the king in a duchy more likely to bear Duke Bedoa's Iron. And there *were* plenty of crests for the mighty border family that was House Iron, its black banner of a forge like a beacon of strength in the history of the nation.

And no doubt due to the size of Minyor, the only two inns bore the Iron Crest.

But the nearest one, the Black Pony, offered lively flute music, and so Anyo entered and paid for lodgings from their dwindling funds. Without even taking a seat, Han bade Binya goodnight and ushered Anyo into one of the rooms, leaving Katonga behind as well.

Barely a glance at the space with its single bed and drawn curtain, and Han had him seated upon the mattress, standing over him with a glare. "No more avoiding my questions, lad. Prince or no, I'll have your attention now or you'll be sorry, understand? You're not so old that I won't put you over my knee like when you were a boy."

Anyo fought off a smile. *This is a lot like back then.* And while his mentor was indeed serious, the image somehow, was not. "You're worried about the promises I made."

"Of course I am," he started, voice rising, but he took a breath. "Forgive me. But this is the first I or Katonga have heard of any rebellion to overthrow your father *and* your brothers, so that *you* can rule. What happened to changing Nasaru?"

"Ruling will make that easier." Deep down, should it have been a surprise? Father was the worst kind of madman; outwardly very reasonable, but cunning and desperate. For years now, he had the city stretched to breaking point with grand visions of beauty and dominance, which he cloaked in comforting lies about security.

Yet what the man wanted was a return to empire.

All the sabre-rattling and hysteria over Senoja spies simply fed the same fire. Not that spies didn't exist, but there was no looming invasion, only the old fool's fetid hopes for one. *Perhaps I always wanted this anyway – to depose him.* "It is the best way to turn the nation around, isn't it? Not to mention restore my honour."

"Madness. We never spoke of deposing, only uniting. Discovering the Sothalic will do that well enough, just like we planned."

"So it might." He met Han's eyes. "But I wonder if that's enough for me now. And even if I did offer my service with the blade to one of my brothers, or even Kiteka, would that be enough? Do they truly believe as I do, that we need to stop war with Senoja? That Takirov should have its independence?"

Han's eyes widened. "What are you saying? Is this because of that corpse-singer?"

"I will honour my word, of course. But no, not truly."

"Meaning?"

"That I don't really know what will happen when I return with the Sothalic. I *could* inspire the whole city. Change things. But I could do more as King."

"Some things can be changed with a blade, I'll admit that, lad. But even if I thought this was a good idea, that wouldn't be all you need."

"I know, of course," Anyo said as he rose. "But can I still count on you and Katonga?"

Han raked a hand through his white hair. "To find the Mirror Blade and to protect you, yes. After that... well. I know your father is not the man *his* father was – not at all, but I want your promise again, that when you change Omaila, you will do it without killing your own kin. Kat may have to answer for himself."

"I will ask him, as prince and friend."

"Friend only, when you get right down to it – Exiled as you are."

"No need to rub salt in the wound," Anyo said with a smile.

Han exhaled. "All jokes aside, I'll need you to swear to me. And Katonga, whenever he joins us."

"I swear it."

Han nodded. "Then let's get some sleep. I'll worry about the rest of it *after* we find the Mirror Blade."

***

Glass shattered.

Anyo sat bolt upright, fumbling for his blade where it lay beside the bed – only for his grip to falter upon the cool steel. In the moonlight, Han and Katonga stood naked upon their bedrolls, necks craned to stare up at the ceiling – motionless and silent.

Gleaming shards of broken glass lay at the foot of the window, no breeze to stir the open curtains – and outside, no hints of someone upon the roof. No-one else in the room either, no traces of attack, not even a stone upon the floor that might explain the glass. "Han? Kat?"

Neither responded.

"Hey!" He rose, staring at them. Nothing. "Answer me, will you?"

Still nothing.

Has someone been here, to do this? Perhaps a Coral Sorcerer? But sent by whom? Anyo stepped into his pants and boots, then took up his blade as he approached the window, glancing out. Below, only shadows and on ground level, a single lamp that cast a small pool of light, painting the cobblestones a soft shade.

Anyo reached for Han then, taking the shorter man by the shoulders. "Han, can you hear me?"

Han was breathing, but his eyes remained wide, unblinking. And instead of pupils, the reflection of a bright moon lay within, a pale-blue fire. Anyo leapt over to Katonga – the same moon within his eyes.

"Kat, please!"

But still nothing. Anyo clenched his jaw. What by all the fickle Gods had happened? *And why was I spared whatever this is?* He started for the door but hesitated. Neither Han nor Katonga seemed visibly hurt or in pain, at least. "If you can hear me, I'll find out what's happened. I'll fix this."

Anyo took the handle and pressed his ear against the door – all calm beyond. He slipped into the dimly-lit corridor. No sinister shadows. A few steps along and he reached out to knock on Binya's door. When he received no answer, he called her name and still nothing.

If she was sleeping, it would not do to simply burst into a lady's room…

Idiot, something is wrong here!

He turned the handle – locked. Anyo stood back and aimed a heavy kick right beside the handle. The door burst open with a crack, splinters falling, and a cry came from the darkened bed. "Binya, it's me. Someone has broken into this place. They've done something to Han and Katonga."

She rose to a half-sitting position, a mere shift of shadows. "I, wait. Anyo? What are you talking about?"

He turned back to the hallway. "Get dressed, and bring your knife at least."

Anyo glanced up and down the passage but found not even a sign of movement. Nor had anyone come to investigate the sound of a door being broken down. Was everyone else frozen?

Had the intruder already moved downstairs? Or into another room perhaps? It had to be a Coral Sorcerer gone mad, surely. *Is that the best you can come up with?* He frowned. Yet Takirov rebels would hardly use mysterious magic to terrorise the people of an inn found inside a modest town such as Minyor…

"What is it?" Binya said when she joined him, wrapped in a dark cloak, knife in hand.

"Look next door, you'll see. They cannot move," Anyo replied, and led her back to his room. "It's their eyes."

Binya strode in and examined their faces closely, frowning as she did. "Even if this were natural, the moon couldn't possibly reflect in their eyes through the roof."

"Exactly." She was taking it better than he had. "Do you know what this is?"

She shook her head.

"Come on, then."

Anyo checked the nearest room and found another man standing tall, motionless, and beside him a small boy, likely his son. Neither responded to Anyo's voice. In the next two rooms, he managed only to startle guests of the Black Pony, and within the third, a woman in a nightgown stood straight and mute as the others, her eyes also bearing only luminous moons… and more, more of her face seemed to be faintly aglow.

He gripped his sword tighter. "Why is it only some of us?"

"I feel something below," Binya said.

Anyo led her to the stairs, sword held ready. Even before he started down, a pale glow, luminous blue or silver – for some reason, he could not be sure of which – emanated from the common room. Whoever had broken into the inn waited below. But what exactly? A sorcerer? Something else? *Can I even face whoever it is with only a sword?*

Turning away from the threat was not going to happen. He gripped his weapon and entered the glow, Binya close behind, taking each step carefully, but the light caused no pain. His limbs did not stiffen into immobility either.

"Are you ready?" he asked Binya.

"For what?" she asked, a touch of bemusement in her voice.

"Good point." Anyo continued down the stair and at bottom, found the night attendant standing in the common room's centre. The man was staring up at the ceiling, hands empty, dustpan and brush at his feet.

The glow in the room actually emanated from his face, a troubling new detail.

Otherwise, the scene offered no answers.

Only two hiding places were available to an intruder – the fireplace and the bar. That, or whoever was responsible for the strange attack on the inn lurked in the kitchen. Or had already gone.

Or maybe, they've possessed the attendant?

"Do you see anything?" Anyo asked Binya.

She shook her head.

Anyo approached the bar, blade raised.

"Just what is the meaning of this?" An irate voice echoed from the stairs, sharp footfalls to go with it.

Anyo spun. One of the guests he'd disturbed earlier? "Do not come down here!"

"Don't you dare tell me what to do," the voice snapped back as a heavy-set fellow stepped into view, his hair and beard unkempt.

"Anyo!" Binya pulled Anyo back to face the bar.

Something white and gleaming rose from the long counter. It could have been a person or a ghost, its skin bearing a glitter, like luminous sand. When it stepped forward, sparkling dust trailed silent movements.

The face was equally unnatural.

Sharp eyes and mouth, all three little more than dark openings... yet did it not seem that something sparkled within? Like stars. And the dark sockets were drawing him *in*. Somehow, the entire sky resided within the creature's eyes...

Wait!

"Do not look into its eyes," he cried out as he tore his gaze free.

The creature continued its gentle approach, trails of glittering sand the only sound now as its feet crossed the floorboards.

"Stop!" Anyo shouted at it.

The thing did not even slow.

He raised his blade and charged, swinging at its neck – but the sharp steel merely passed through the body with a gentle hiss. He attacked again, slicing through hands and torso, anything but the face...

The creature did not falter. It barely lost its shape as it *reformed* around the deep slashes. Anyo pivoted to swing again, but pale arms shot out and caught him by the shoulders now, dragging him close without a word.

Anyo squeezed his eyes shut as the face loomed.

A chill bled into his body, long fingers burning his flesh with ice. He thrashed against the cold even as his limbs stiffened, and despite the brush of grains against his cheeks, like a breath of snow, he still would not open his eyes.

But it was a losing battle. Whether his eyes were open or closed, the cold would freeze him, and his sword was useless.

A long, harsh scream shattered the quiet.

Binya?

Cold vanished and he opened one eye slowly, squinting at... darkness. Only a faint glow rose from his feet; a small pile of luminous sand mixed of silver, white and faint traces of blue also. The longer he stared, mouth slightly agape, the easier it was to find pricks of gold resting within the pile.

Binya put a hand on his arm. "Anyo?"

"I can move," he eventually said. He exhaled, relief causing him to tremble, meeting her worried gaze. "Thank you. I...

How did you know your voice would work?"

"I didn't. I just tried whatever came to mind – like you." She shrugged. "Maybe it was surprised? Somehow, I doubt I destroyed… whatever that was."

She was right, and there no way to be sure. But one thing remained absolutely certain; the creature had been far too powerful.

"W-what was that t-thing?"

Anyo turned to where the rotund patron had fallen against the wall, tears streaming down his face now.

"We do not know," he told the man, speaking gently. "Best you head back to your room, in case it returns."

"Yes, yes," the man said as he scrambled for the stairs.

"His question stands," Binya observed, and her own jaw seemed to be clenched.

"So it does." Anyo glanced back down at the pile of sand, now far less luminous, and nearby, the attendant who had collapsed… unconscious, chest rising and falling gently. "But I want to check on Han and Katonga. And the rest of the inn first. Maybe your voice broke its spell for everyone."

"I hope so."

CHAPTER 27. – ANYO

Both Han and Katonga were free from the creature's spell, already dressed and armed when Anyo and Binya met them upstairs. After hearing what had happened, and checking on the pile of mysterious sand below, neither felt it prudent to stay the rest of the night.

Han grunted. "If for no other reason than the local people potentially seeking to blame travellers for what happened, we should leave."

"Agreed," Anyo replied. "Let's see if we can…"

He trailed off as Binya knelt beside the pile of sand, a mug taken from the table now in her hand. She scooped up some of the sand, barely glimmering at all now, then moved to the bar and rummaged around a moment. When she returned, it was with a piece of cloth and string, which she used to seal the mug.

"Isn't that dangerous?" Katonga asked.

She nodded. "Probably. But I wonder if a Coral Sorcerer can offer some answers."

"In case we encounter that thing again?" Anyo asked.

"Or in case there's more than one of them."

Han nodded. "Anything seems possible now."

Footsteps and voices were gathering upstairs.

"Time to go." Anyo led them from the Black Pony and through the village streets at a brisk walk. There, they passed a few people in their nightclothes, stumbling back toward their doors... had they been caught too? He glanced up at the moon; a bright orb that offered no answers.

Even the western gate stood open, the gate guard mumbling to himself as he worked to close it once more. Anyo hailed the fellow. "Isn't the gate usually closed of an evening?"

The guard wiped at his brow, offering a generally unfriendly glance. "So it ought to be, why?"

"I merely found it unusual. Is something amiss, here?"

Now the man folded his arms. "No."

"But you opened the gate yourself?" Han asked. "Did someone leave before us?"

"Not that I remember." He shrugged, frown now seeming to be directed at himself. He had a hand on his heavy cudgel. "Fact is, I don't believe I opened the gate myself just before – no reason to have done that. Sebak must have forgotten earlier."

"I see. We'll be on our way, then," Anyo said.

"Hurry it along."

And then the village of Minyor was behind them, and with it the luminous creature... perhaps.

The moon-lit road stretched alongside farmland – dark fields of swaying crops and silent homes, the cobbles empty of travellers or confused village-folk alike.

Was there a limit to the sand-creature's influence, then? *Or the people have already recovered.* Either way, answers were not forthcoming. To the far west, in the distant land of Viareya, there were supposedly Siren Shades able to charm a person for a time, but nothing like what had appeared at the inn.

Not even in myth or legend could Anyo come up with anything similar.

Should I have sent word to House Iron's sorcerers, asking them to investigate?

For if the fiend of sand was not alone, or not actually defeated at all... He turned to Binya who walked beside him. "Your voice stopped it back there. Are there any stories from the south, perhaps, that could describe that thing?"

She shook her head slowly. "Not that I know of."

"Anyone we might ask?"

"Not from here." She shook her head. "Our best chance is a Coral Sorcerer, as I said. Isn't it?"

"Doubtless," he replied.

"Then we're at the mercy of Dibora for answers," she said. "And faster transportation, I imagine, since if nothing else, your impatience suggests you're concerned."

"I am."

Binya raised a hand. "Not that I'm saying you shouldn't be – after all, I'm carrying part of that thing myself, so I want to know as much as you. But isn't it most likely to be a mistake, a result of some magic gone awry? Perhaps a damaged sorcerer trying to live out some... I don't know, some mad grudge against the town or the inn? Even someone staying there? After all, we know nothing of the place."

"Possibly." Anyo glanced up at the moon. It was still glaring down at them, and it could have been a mere fancy, but did the shadows upon its surface have the look of a leer? "But what if it is something worse, somehow?"

"I suppose that's part of why I'm carrying the sand."

"Kat, what do you think?" Anyo asked.

In an almost comical way, the man was walking with arms crossed. "There are no stories about such a thing here in the west."

"And?"

"And so I'd like to suggest we post a watch in pairs this night."

Han nodded his agreement.

By the time they made camp in a somewhat damp hollow beside the road, and sought their rest once more, neither Binya nor anyone else had come up with a single satisfactory theory to explain the creature.

When sleep came, it was fitful… but better than nothing.

Once the cool morning broke, clouds overstaying their welcome above as the group set out, the task of finding horses at Dibora became more pressing. The thin purse at his belt was a clear reminder of the difficulties ahead. Notwithstanding, even if the jewels he'd hidden away in the caves above the capital had been on hand, all had been promised to Binya. The last of his wealth. *But they are worthless if I cannot use them to do something meaningful.*

Finding the Sothalic would have to be enough to start change.

"I suppose we could steal some horses. Find a way to pay back whoever it is when we pass through on the way home?" Katonga suggested.

Han's deep frown quickly established the older man's response to the suggestion.

"Best used as a last resort, perhaps," Anyo replied. "After all, we have nothing to barter with. And even here to the west, I'm sure all have heard of the Beggar Prince."

Katonga sighed. "Hence my suggestion… but there is another possibility. Not my first choice, I suppose, but it might work."

"Yes?"

"Dibora is no small town and it does boast at least one fine brothel."

Anyo raised an eyebrow. "Ah, what are you suggesting, Kat?"

The man grinned. "I'm a man of hidden talents."

Han sighed.

"I see… well, I don't think I'd ask you to do that as a first choice, either," Anyo said. "But if you're willing, I will rely on those hidden talents." He gave Katonga a look. "We've been short of gold before, you know. Why now?"

"We haven't spent all that much time in the west. And there are several places in these parts that I have been able to command a high price in the past. I'm not *that* much older now, so I'd expect similar success, if necessary."

Binya too, was appraising him. "Four horses. That's not going to be a single night's toil."

"Certainly not. But we have no particular time-limit," he replied, his voice calm, and in fact, his entire bearing unconcerned. "If it's needed of me, I will do my best."

Anyo had no answer at first. *He is certainly blessed with more confidence than I.* "Kat, thank you. Let us see what awaits us in Dibora before we decide."

***

Unlike the walls surrounding Minyor, Dibora's walls were of stone, but within, the far larger town seemed as sparsely populated… which made little sense. Dibora offered at least half a dozen inns, a public bathhouse, small speciality markets of semi-precious stones or bright hangings of cloth, and detailed artworks of charcoal. Even a park with green lawns for games of Square Toss favoured by nobles – but the paved streets were hushed.

Few townsfolk visited stalls or shopkeepers of any ilk, and most that did regarded Anyo and his companions with narrowed eyes or furtive glances.

The central market, unlike the others, was arranged in a circle and stood only a little less empty. Perhaps a third of the stalls were open but with few people moving between them, and those who attended hurried off after conducting their business. The place seemed emptier than it truly was.

The shopkeepers and stallholders waited without welcoming expressions, some even pacing. One fruit seller was already packing her wares away despite the noon hour.

Had something dark occurred in the town?

"This is becoming more than odd." Anyo came to a halt before an empty platform in the centre of the square. In times less tense, a vendor ought to have been given pride of place but today, there was no fortunate – or already wealthy – merchant that had been permitted to set up a stall. Instead, an old timer sat upon the surface, a begging bowl between his mismatched shoes, pile of twigs in hand.

"For a coin, I would be more than willing to answer any questions you might have," the beggar offered. His voice did not hold out much hope.

"About why everyone seems uncomfortable here?" Anyo asked.

"Yes, My Lord."

Anyo reached for a small denomination but paused. "I am no lord."

The old man bowed his head. "Of course. Forgive any insult. You simply have that look about you."

"Then anything you can share would be appreciated. Starting with why it is so quiet, here."

"The ghost is why."

"Ghost?"

"Aye. The Pale Walker, supposedly. Heard Sosu call it a sand-wraith, but who knows? Whatever name we give it, doesn't seem that important."

Anyo hesitated. *Here too?*

"You don't seem convinced?" Han asked the fellow.

"Well, I will say that I doubt it's a ghost. Something else is afoot, something worse. Most likely some Coral Sorcerer has gone and got himself all Salt Sick and done something he shouldn't have, and *that's* why some people have just disappeared. Some of the lucky ones have stopped talking altogether, now that they've been found." He paused. "And not because they can't talk no longer, I reckon. But because they won't. They don't *want* to talk about what happened."

Anyo leant closer. "Do any know what happened to them?"

He nodded. "Near enough, I'd think. Some people are found just standing still, gazing up to the sky. Can't speak and don't move unless they're carried. Every morning now, we find more folks missing. Or refusing to talk. Town fathers have called in all sorts over the past couple of weeks, pleaded with the duke for help, but so far, nothing makes a difference."

"Not even other Coral Sorcerers?" Katonga asked.

"It's been happening for weeks?" Han asked at the same time.

The old-timer rubbed at white stubble. "It has. And so far, no Coral Sorcerer has made any difference."

"But you're not afraid?" Binya asked.

"If my life was worth losing, I'd have something to worry about." He tossed one of the twigs to the stones. "And that's all I know, strangers. Now it's your turn, and don't be afraid to be generous with your donation."

Anyo offered two small coins instead of the one he had originally planned. It would not help them afford horses, but on the other hand, the fellow *had* been helpful. "Who might be able to tell us more?"

"Sosu, the innkeeper at the Green Broom," he replied as he used one coin to tap against the other, as if to test their authenticity. "But if you ask me, it seems strange for travellers such as yourselves to take an interest."

"We saw similar things in Minyor," Anyo replied. "It was not something we could forget, and we hope to avoid it here."

Now the beggar shrugged. "Then best you hurry on and see Sosu. Left at the jeweller. You'll see the dying tree, down that way. Past the dome."

Anyo thanked him and led the way across the square and into streets lined with homes that featured little carvings of anvils on their doors, or warding symbols painted on the windows. A single person walked ahead, arms laden with loaves of bread. They quickened their step before turning into a temple whose twin sets of diamond-shaped windows were darkened by closed curtains.

Unwelcoming. The western sect of Aehtu had a reputation as quiet but caring... Katonga would probably know more. Most of the other shops and homes were similarly empty or closed off. Perhaps the sect was simply following the supposed prevailing wisdom of the town: stay indoors.

But beyond the jeweller – also closed – there waited a large dome, set off from the street in a little garden. As in other larger towns and cities, the stone monument had been carved with small faces and names, arranged in rows. Usually, the date of the Second Coral War ran around the highest rung, but it was the three figures standing nearby that drew Anyo's attention.

They did not turn or hurry away.

Each wore dark-yellow cloaks and hoods, with the tallest being flanked by shorter figures; two women, perhaps, both of whom carried bows across their shoulders, and quivers at their hips.

The taller figure wore a two-pronged spear strapped to his back.

He did not reach for it as Anyo led the others closer; rather, he pushed his hood back to reveal a smiling face, close-cropped beared covering some of his tanned skin.

Cresidethians?

A little far from home. The contrasting nation of desert and jungle was a week by ship, and that was after you reached the coast. Few travellers or merchants ventured between the nations, or, at least, few who did moved much farther than the first port.

What were they doing in Dibora?

"*Inithora-fal*. Greetings," the man said. "We are pleased to meet you here. Perhaps you can help us?" Though his accent was strong, his words were deliberate enough that Anyo understood.

"We are travellers ourselves," Anyo replied. "Perhaps a local?"

"Certainly, but so few seem willing to leave their homes." The Cresidethian gestured to his companions. "I am Nuvin and these are my sisters, Elin and Fiana. We have travelled from afar seeking *your* aid."

He frowned. "*My* aid?"

"You are Prince Anyo."

Anyo placed a hand upon the hilt of his blade but did not draw. Beside him, Han, Katonga and even Binya straightened, but the Cresidethians did not react to the movements. "I do not believe we have crossed paths before, Nuvin."

The man raised both hands. "We have not, yet I have been seeking you for some time. You are uniquely suited to our quest, you see."

"Being?"

"Saving the lands from a darkness quite eternal," he replied, his cheer fading. "I believe you have already encountered its slaves, considering what your Takirov companion carries with her."

CHAPTER 28. – ANYO

"That does not lend you much credence, Nuvin," Anyo replied. He had not drawn, though nor did he loosen his grip. The stranger hardly appeared close to striking… but on the other hand, could he be trusted? "After all, who else but someone involved with these so-called slaves could recognise the sand concealed upon another's person?"

"Please –"

"Further, your claim that you know of me seems further suspect. We will be on our way."

Nuvin took half a step closer, hands raised. "Forgive me, I admit some theatrics to arrest your attention but our concern is true. We believe that you, the so-called Beggar Prince, are the only one who can recover the Sothalic – and the Sothalic is *dearly* needed in the struggle against darkness."

Anyo exchanged a glance with Han before narrowing his gaze at the stranger. "How do you know of the Sothalic?"

"All in Cresideth know of the famous Mirror Blade gifted to your ancestors by our Zenith."

Anyo shook his head. "No, stranger. What I am asking, is how do you know that *I* am searching for it? And how did you find me?"

"Please, you can call me Nuvin. If you wish, we can discuss this over a meal at The Regal. We have rooms there."

"It is quiet enough right here," Han said, his sizeable arms folded over his chest.

"Certainly, Han of Omaila. Your prudence is worthy." He motioned to his sisters, who knelt and removed their packs.

"You know us all, then?"

Nuvin nodded. "Again, please consider trusting us once you have heard what we have to say. My abilities are disconcerting for most, but at least take some lorimir with us and decide whether you will accept our assistance."

The sisters worked swiftly to construct small benches of folding steel, obviously designed in such a way to be carried. Nuvin went to his own pack then, withdrawing five cups and two thin vials of a bright-pink liquid.

He poured five drinks, the liquid sliding free slowly, then addressed everyone. "I apologise for not having enough cups. We will take no offence if some of you do not wish to try the lorimir. It is a sweet, ceremonial fruit drink, for sipping only. I warn you, as it is often too much for southerners."

Anyo eased his hand from his sword. The Cresidethians seemed to know more than should have been possible. Especially for travellers. How long had they been in Nasaru? What were the abilities Nuvin mentioned? *Exactly who are these people?* "I will drink, if that is your custom," Anyo eventually said.

"And I," Binya added quickly. "I have heard of lorimir but never did I expect to be able to try it."

"Certainly," Nuvin said with a smile, handing two cups

across.

"I'm just as curious about the benches you manage to carry around," Katonga said.

One of the sisters, Anyo had already forgotten which, grinned. "We do not take meals upon the earth unless necessary."

"I see," Katonga replied, though his brow was furrowed.

Nuvin lifted his cup and spoke a Cresi phrase before taking a sip. He exhaled after, a smile upon his face.

Anyo followed suit, and the moment the liquid hit his tongue, he gasped. So sweet as to burn! Yet the discomfort did not last, and a fleeting aftertaste followed. Almost like... strawberry and raspberry combined? Such description was inadequate.

Binya had already taken another sip, the lorimir apparently to her liking.

"Your hospitality aside, I am still loath to trust you. I find myself very interested in exactly how you learned of me and my quest," Anyo asked, nursing the cup. "You have my attention."

The man nodded. "As I said, all know of the Sothalic but it falls to our line to watch for the days when it will be needed once more. Here in the south, I would be called a sorcerer. But my role is perhaps just as close to a diplomat crossed with… a monk, as you might know such people? We are called Femithir, and one gift given to my ancestors is that we can communicate with animals. What they see, we see, and more, what they remember, we remember. This is especially true for owls, whose wisdom goes far beyond ours."

Anyo met the man's unfaltering gaze. It was certainly an explanation, and while it seemed a little more sophisticated than what Cresideth people were said to be able to do, that did not make Nuvin a liar. *He knows not only specific details about what I'm looking for, but* where *to find us.*

If nothing else, the Femithir were indeed diplomats.

Han raised an eyebrow but his question was not about Nuvin's powers. "If your line watches for a time when the Sothalic will be needed, then why give it away in the first place?"

Nuvin rubbed at his chin. "Perhaps my ancestors had their doubts, but there is a reason – one beyond that of diplomacy."

Han frowned. "Nothing comes to mind, if you are waiting for a guess."

Nuvin smiled. "No need. It is simply that your lands are where the darkness was defeated last, and where it may very well awaken again."

"There is a flaw in that plan," Katonga observed.

"Certainly. We know, as do you of course, that the Mirror Blade has been lost for many, many years. That had not mattered precisely, at least, not so long as the great threat lay dormant. But all the animals upon the land speak of the old malice stirring once more, deep beneath the earth. Thankfully, we have enough time to act."

"Then what of this darkness?" Anyo asked.

"His true name is unknown, but the name that has been passed down to me was Wethucirsa. Moon Father, in your language."

"It is not a name I have ever heard," Anyo said, and the others shook their heads.

"His name in any language is a warning. The powerful shadow we are striving to fight is no symbolic threat, either – you have seen his minions. The Moon Father will cloak the sun in black clouds. Forever. Light will slip through, but not enough for all life. Not enough for healthy crops. Not enough for healthy children. In time, only *his* children will remain. Of a day, they will lurk, and at night they will walk, strengthened by the moon in numbers too vast for us to stand against," he said, tone grave. "Assuming we can even exist after the sun has been banished."

Anyo did not answer at once.

A darkness that eventually strangled all life? Hordes of pale things, the sand-walkers... was it truly possible? Did Wethucirsa actually exist? "That is a troubling tale. It is difficult to imagine, however."

"Diplomatically stated, Your Highness," Nuvin replied. "But you need not take my word for it. You have already encountered his Children in the moonlight."

Han and Katonga exchanged a glance.

"It somehow entranced people," Anyo said after a moment. "Not everyone, but we could not make them respond."

"Yes. If given enough time, the Children devour those they catch, using their bodies as strength gained to spawn more Children."

"You are well-informed about these Children," Han observed.

Nuvin frowned. "I understand you will have doubts, but the less than subtle insinuation once more that we are *responsible* for the horrors of the Children is not appreciated."

Han did not continue, nor did he offer any manner of apology.

Anyo raised a hand to forestall further tension or insult. Nuvin and his sisters were probably at least worth listening to. Their claims about the coming darkness, the Moon Father and Sothalic could be tested, or at least some claims could be tested easily enough. "Tell us, how could the Sothalic help?

My blade had no effect on the… 'Child' we encountered."

"The Mirror Blade is forged of the moon – its celestial silver will cut down our enemies. That is what is written in the oldest Femithir tomes, the very reason my sisters and I have found you."

Anyo leant forward. "Even so, it is only one blade."

Nuvin gestured to his sisters. "With the Sothalic, we could forge more. It is what Elin and Fiana have trained for all their lives, just as our mother did before them. Yet if the Sothalic is used to pierce the still-awakening Moon Father in his tomb, then new forgings will not be needed."

"If all of what you claim is true, why exactly do you require my help? You could simply seek out the sword yourselves."

"Of all the princes of the land, you are the one already seeking the Sothalic. You need no convincing to search, and when it is found, you will be able to mobilise your people, if needed." He glanced at Han. "Could you imagine if someone such as myself, a stranger from Cresideth, attempted to rally the people here, using a Nasaru royal artefact?"

Han frowned.

A fair point. "Yet I am no prince, now," Anyo said.

"A small detail, and easily rectified once you return triumphant – which is your own goal, or so the birds have told me."

"A small detail?" And how exactly did the birds know such things, and communicate it to Nuvin? Anyo handed back the cup. "We will consider your offer of assistance."

"That is most gracious, Your Highness. We will await you in this place."

Anyo led Han and the others across the street to stop

before a closed butcher, distant enough that whispering would not be necessary. He glanced around for birds or even mice, any small animal...

But before he could ask any questions of them, Binya spoke. "If you wish, I could seek to read Nuvin. I don't believe it necessary, but if he holds any dark secrets, you will know whether he can be trusted. If he refuses, it could be argued that he has something he wishes to keep from us."

"You can also read the living?"

She nodded. "Not with such detail as the dead, no. But enough to form an opinion."

"Well, that might be needed," Anyo said. "What of you, Han? Katonga, I know you've actually travelled to Cresideth once before."

"I have," he replied, glancing back toward Nuvin and his sisters, who were drinking from their sweet cups. "Femithir are revered there, though I met none in the port city of Daviinor. I know little else. It does seem that they could prove useful allies... if they can be trusted."

"Han?"

"I'll be watching them, should we travel together. And it is your decision, lad, but I will say that if these Pale Walkers or Children or whatever they are proven to be, are a threat on the scale he describes, then that Femithir seems to know a lot more than we do." The older man sighed. "And after all, what use is returning from exile to an empire of darkness and death?"

"Then you believe it is possible, what he is claiming?"

"Well... whether a creature called the Moon Father exists and is really about to wake, I don't know. But we know those

Pale Walkers are real." His expression darkened. "And since it wasn't just one in that inn, it seems likely we'll meet more."

"You don't believe there's a chance it's a Coral Sorcerer behind this, after all? Or a group of them?"

"Do you, lad?"

Anyo shook his head after a moment. "I do not, no."

"There's one more reason," Binya added. "Strength in numbers."

Katonga nodded. "And if they've taken rooms at The Regal, they're well-funded."

"Very well," Anyo said with a small smile at Kat's practicality. "Let's take them with us."

CHAPTER 29. – ROKURA

In his room at the Quiet House, with a new, somewhat thinner cloak of black settled across his shoulders, Rokura smiled; perhaps the colour was too obvious. *Mourning what I have lost?* No. Mourning for the Code, which was suddenly crumbling even as he strapped on a belt with cheaper knives and a purse – containing whatever coins Cosequ could spare.

He wrenched at the belt when it caught on a loop. Maybe the smile was a bitter one, aimed at his own naivety. Or pride. And sadness. *After all, you believed that to follow the Code was to place yourself above the whims of the corrupt.* He shook his head. *It only made you easy to sweep aside.*

Yet the question remained – swept aside from what? And by whom?

Duke Bedoa? *Either he knows I am on his trail, or he is striking at the king for other reasons… which might just mean that the princess is involved?* Or that was merely a wild, fanciful suspicion borne out of bitterness.

Rokura sighed. Whatever the truth, it was not something he would discover any time soon.

Cosequ looked up from where he leant upon the windowsill,

staring down into the busy street, the murmur of voices seeming rather close. "Are you still going to help that young man now? Even if the rumours are only half true, even if you find the Mistress and he gets some clue or by some miracle actual help, what will you do then?"

"Exactly what I was doing before. Find Brutan and save the young ones."

Cosequ straightened with a frown. "Wait a moment. How? And more importantly, why? You don't need to do that anymore. You're free, if you want to look at it that way. And more, you'll be Executed if you interfere. This feels like you're trying to win back the cloak."

"No." That wasn't... Rokura opened his mouth to continue but stopped. Was his cousin right? *No, it's not quite that.* But Cosequ wasn't entirely wrong either. "That young man – all of the children who have been captured, they all deserve to be rescued."

"If they're even alive by the time you find them."

"I will know the truth," Rokura said, lowering his voice.

Cosequ sighed. "I'm not surprised, cousin."

"No?"

"No. I'm almost proud, if you can accept that." He spread his hands. "But you'd better take that strange boy and leave the city now, before the princess or that merchant's friends come after you. No consequences for them taking your life, now that you're no longer a Greyshield *or* a noble, remember?"

"That's why you're helping me pack," Rokura replied. "And, I hope, you will uncover the truth about the governor, at least."

"That much I promise."

He crossed the room to embrace the man. "Thank you."

"I owe you for half a dozen moments during our childhood when you saved me, if nothing else," Cosequ replied with a grin. He handed over Rokura's pack. "Now, get going, quickly."

Rokura left with a growing weight in his chest but found Iggy in the next room and had them out the door and to the stable and then into the streets swiftly.

I don't think I understand what has happened now, either, Iggy said as they crossed the street, making way for a line of wagons, and headed for the southern gate, which loomed above the crowds. *I feel like I am saying that a lot.*

Rokura reached out to rest a hand on the lad's shoulder. "All nations are like this, with rules that can be broken by the powerful. But can you say you fully understood your home?"

Yes. Which is why I left, Rokura.

Not the answer he'd been expecting. "Then let me simply say, I still believe in something... but I no longer believe that my former role is the only place that thing can be found."

Well, that I think I understand.

"And what of your own quest? Were you able to find a clue, searching from your room?"

"Nuka guided me, in the end. And now that we are close enough, I can feel the Mistress myself – in the woods to the south."

Rokura nodded slowly. Somehow, the fact that the Mistress of Obsidian was not only real but still living, was diminished by his overall dour mood. So too, the ease with which she had been located. "Then I will accompany you to her."

Thank you, Rokura.

It did not take long after passing Atanoph, following the road through more pale plains and sparse stands of trees, before Rokura drew his horse to a halt. Three figures stepped from a grove. All were armed. Two held swords and one man, the biggest, carried a mace with sharpened flanges that glinted in the sunlight.

None wore the Grey, nor any recognisable House Crest, nor the armour and red tabard of the royal soldiers. Just dark, plain clothing.

By their flat expressions, they approached with no cheerful welcome in mind.

"You do not have any business with me. Leave now if you value your lives," Rokura said with a growl.

The lead man, his face thin and wary, stepped back, but the big guy leant down to speak into the leader's ear with a frown. "Steady. Who cares what he *was*, right? There's three of us."

"Do you think that matters?" Rokura raised his voice.

The leader spat, then charged.

Rokura whipped a blade free – and a blinding flash followed.

He flinched over Arrow's neck, blinking furiously. When he could see once more, their attackers lay prone upon the highway. All three seemed to be breathing, but when Rokura dismounted and approached, giving the leader a kick, the man did not stir.

He glanced over his shoulder. "Iggy?"

The young man nodded. *They don't seem to be dead. I'm happy with that.*

"You mean, you're happy with your control?"

Yes. If I'm not careful, I could kill easily – and even if they were obviously not friendly, I didn't want them dead.

A heartening revelation. And yet, that might have been unkind. After all, Iggy's determination did not have to equate to heartless slaughter. "Let's move quickly then, the light could have attracted attention."

Right.

Rokura led them on until nightfall, finding a serviceable campsite within the woods, and set about clearing the earth while Iggy used a nearby creek to drink.

When the tents were up and water boiling over a small fire-pit, Rokura rested against a trunk to stare into the darkness. Beyond, the distant road was still just visible through the trees via pale glimpses. For the most part, merchants and their swaying lamps passed only occasionally, or the hoof-beats of travellers, until it was just the echo of hooves and no lights, and finally naught but the wind…

Rokura woke with a start.

He groaned as he shot to his feet, limbs creaking. Falling asleep while on watch like a damned novice? Nearby, ashes in the campfire sat cold and grey beneath a dawn sky. *Well, isn't that a fine little dagger in my side?* Yet there was no time for further recrimination or morose grumbling. Iggy was gone. Rokura spun. Had something happened? The camp was not unshielded, but there was still a chance they'd been followed…

I'm here.

Iggy was walking through the trees, clothes damp. From behind him, the soft call of running water.

"Ah."

So, you fell asleep, did you? It seemed Iggy could have been smiling.

"To my considerable shame, yes."

We may not need to watch each night, not with Nuka. She can watch over us.

Rokura resisted the urge to frown. "Is that so?"

Don't worry. I said I have an idea for when we reach the Mistress, remember?

"I do," he replied as he leant once more against the bark. "And now seems as good a time as any to tell me about it."

Iggy sat by the fire-pit and started to roll up his blanket. *Nuka believes that my gift should be strong enough to withstand the Mistress – and that the Mistress will be curious enough to listen. Nuka said no-one ever goes near her, and that the Mistress might even be happy to lure us into her home, if nothing else. That's my chance.*

"That's..." Rokura sighed. "That's not a plan. That's suicide."

There is more.

"Good."

The Mistress might be able to help me – at a cost, of course. She wants something beneath the ocean, but someone like me can retrieve it.

Vague. Yet setting aside more than a few issues, Iggy was probably correct about being able to complete such a feat. The search was its own course of insanity, nevertheless. And above all, why did Nuka want to help Iggy? *How* did the creature know so much about the Mistress of Obsidian?

"Iggy, what does Nuka want in return for helping you?"

Life.

Rokura shuddered at the echo of Nuka's touch, the warmth as she lulled him toward acceptance of an early death. "Life?"

Yes. In exchange for her guidance, I need to help Nuka return to life. We will ask the Mistress of Obsidian.

"This could all too easily become a deadly disaster. If the Mistress does hold all the answers, in order to succeed in your own goal, you must first complete a task for her Mistress. Then you must complete another task, this time on behalf of Nuka, in order to fulfil your debt."

Yes.

"And if everything goes according to plan, what will you have unleashed upon the lands? What will Nuka do with her new life? What will the Mistress do with her deep-sea gift, whatever it may be?"

That I do not know.

"But you will risk great suffering of others for your own goal?"

Iggy folded his arms. *I can only decide that after I meet her for myself. Before that, I am aware I may not be able to* complete *her task to begin with. I don't even know if she* can *help.* He paused. *Perhaps not even the Mistress of Obsidian can give me a face – it is* a desperate gamble.

"So it is," Rokura said with a sigh. Once again, it was clear that Iggy was probably wiser than his years might have suggested. Still, the risks were many…

Then, have you made your own decision?

"I will accompany you to the lair of the witch, as promised."

Thank you.

CHAPTER 30. – ROKURA

The path leading to the abode of the Mistress was overgrown with wild grasses and mossy shrubs, but pleasant enough. Some plants were dotted with wild roses of yellow or white and from the shady trees above, the sweet sound of birdsong echoed. Even the bright blue sky seemed so perfectly pleasant.

It's almost impossible to feel any dread. Rokura sighed. *Ridiculous.*

He came to a halt at a fork in the trail. Both choices simply continued deeper into the wood, like shaded alleyways of bark. Here, the elms were joined by thinner trees. These bore a faint purple tint to smooth bark; the material used by Takirov artists. *How is that poor man faring now?*

"What do you sense, Iggy?"

Only that we must travel deeper. She is waiting.

"Very well." It was hard to believe that such a beautiful place could hide one of the most feared creatures of history. Was the pleasant wood merely the first part of her deception?

As the sun drifted down to a warm dusk, the first real hint of the danger that lay ahead became clear. Foraging for kindling, a branch snagged on something within a tangle of vines. Rokura knelt to tear at them, uncovering the wreckage of a human ribcage. Half-buried by time, the exposed ribs were mostly covered in moss, with little that could be described as white.

Once camp had been set up and a meal of dried meat and toasted bread finished, Rokura asked about Nuka once more.

"Can she tell us anything else about the Mistress?"

I don't know if she will, only that the Mistress is close. I've come to believe they must know each other, however.

"That seems likely." He leant forward. "Are you certain you can trust what you have been told?"

Her desire to return to life is sincere. And as for the Mistress, what use am I to her dead? She must give her instructions.

Rokura sighed. "If it is all not some ruse."

I don't believe so, but only tomorrow will tell. Iggy rose and prepared his bedding, shivering as he did so. From the absence of the sun, or some other reason, Rokura did not ask. Instead, he settled into his own tent to wait for sleep.

***

Nuka had been correct; the lair had been close.

Light poured in from the vast opening in the canopy where Rokura found himself standing before a fallen tree trunk – a fallen monster – so large that it was easily four-storeys tall. Its bark was grey and black, as if it had turned to stone. No branches, no leaves, just an enormous wall of tree trunk rising from equally blasted earth.

For even at the point where the trunk seemed to grow from the ground, the dirt and thin grass was dark too, scattered with ashes and charcoal.

More, a veritable lake of ash rested before the trunk, lying still and fathomless.

This is... an unnatural place. Iggy knelt where the uneven road simply vanished within.

"I agree."

Was it evidence of the tremendous battle from the past? Ash and char should have long-since disappeared but the legendary battle could have happened mere days ago, based upon the lake of grey.

He glanced up at the fallen trunk. There were few small openings, thin or twisted along the length of the ancient tree, but no way to enter from the side. Was it truly her lair? If the lake could be crossed, maybe then they could seek another entry point. Perhaps the root system was gone, allowing access there.

She is within. Waiting to see what we will do.

Rokura glanced down at Iggy. "You can sense her intentions now?"

He nodded.

"Is she planning to attack?"

It doesn't feel like she is... But I've come this far.

"Then we go together," Rokura replied. And it was easier to say than expected. *Because I can't sense the Mistress? Am I still actually in doubt that she's real?* Iggy had sensed *something* within, but what exactly?

The environment did not help. Even with the unusual ash, the tranquil forest and the old tree... nothing seemed to speak of evil precisely. *And what if that is simply part of her ploy.* Rokura nearly shook his head.

Iggy nodded. *Thank you, once more.*

Rokura stepped from the trail a moment, then found a

suitable fallen branch. Next, he approached the ash, using the branch to probe the depths – only a foot or so. "We should be able to walk it," he said.

It does get deeper.

"I'll carry you if need be," Rokura said as he started in. The ashes swirled around his boots, rising like mist, and it did not take long to reach his calves, each step now coming at the cost of a slight drag.

Beside him, Iggy was already up to his knees.

When they reached the middle of the lake, Rokura was wiping sweat from his brow, and the surface had reached his waist. The sun was not so high nor hot... was the ash itself actually warm? Its scent was growing strong too, and Iggy was fighting for each step now. The lad also bore sweat upon his brow. Only *far* more sweat since the ash had reached his chest.

"I'll need to carry you if it gets any deeper," he said. "Or hotter."

Iggy stopped. *Then you feel it too?*

"It's getting easier to see why people stay away from this place. Ready?"

I am.

Rokura rested the branch against his hip then reached down into the ash, heat swimming across his hands and arms, catching a hold of Iggy. The lad was too heavy at first, but the moment Rokura lifted him clear, Iggy's more delicate weight returned. As if the lake had clung to the lad, trying to keep a hold.

"This must be dangerous for you," Rokura said.

Too much and I think I'll suffocate.

"Climb onto my back, then," he said.

When Iggy was settled, Rokura resumed dragging

himself through the ash, using the branch once more. It did not take long before he found another slope and the lake deepened further.

He strode on until the ashes reached his own chest, yet despite the suffocating warmth that grew, the sweat that spread across his entire body now, once he passed the centre, the tail began to climb.

And this time, as the surface of the lake started to fall away, the sense of clinging ash grew. "No," he told it, and wrenched his hips free, almost kicking through the final half of the soot and ash now, even managing a jog by the time the lake's surface had fallen to his ankles.

The extra effort stirred grey clouds, and a thick, bitterness coated his tongue as he coughed, but they were finally free. Iggy hopped down and waved at the lingering clouds.

Rokura leant back against the massive tree trunk; it was colder than expected, soothing against his sweating torso as he caught his breath. "Does the ash still bother you?"

Not as much but it interferes with my vision.

"What about water?"

I could use a little. Iggy removed his pack and knelt to search within, lifting one of three flasks. He then unscrewed the water and tipped some into his cupped palm. And though Rokura had seen it before, the way the water simply disappeared, as though Iggy's skin drank it up, was mesmerising.

Iggy repeated the process twice more, careful not to waste even a single drop due to haphazard pouring. He replaced the lid with a slight slumping of his shoulders, perhaps equivalent to a sigh.

Rokura took a drink from his own flask then reached out

to touch the old bark. "We should probably search its length for a way to enter."

Actually, I can break a hole right here.

It could be just as easy, but would it upset or enrage the Mistress within? Rokura hesitated.

It might bother her. But I think it's more important to show her my power. Iggy said. *She should know that we will not be easily cowed – Nuka agrees.*

Rokura smiled. "Then let me give you some room."

CHAPTER 31. – MEI

The long stair leading down to the port was filled with people climbing past Mei, heading in the opposite direction, up toward the city. Some were burdened by baskets of fish or crabs, while others pulled wheeled carts up the ramp, the most successful among them able to have beasts of burden do the hard work.

The slope wasn't so steep. Landings had been cut into the stair, some with stone benches. Mamalo explained each landing could be used to rest at or trade from, and yet it still seemed a long, inconvenient trip from the enormous blue and green of the harbour for traders to reach the markets.

And the sea was just so vast... stretching beyond her eye, her mind, her imagination. She hadn't even realised, on the way to Giloam at least, that it was a coastal city. Even the towering ships with their pale yellow or white sails seemed so small, almost like toys, compared to the ocean.

How far is the island? She'd asked in the coffee house, and Mamalo explained but the words didn't mean much – a better question would have been how *long* it would take, but Onolse and Nata had rushed them from the room and started the small group to work on gathering provisions.

Mei tried to help, simply by carrying things to and from Nata's horse, but everyone else seemed to have all the details under control. Even with her bone earring, there were times where words and decisions flowed too quickly for her to keep up.

She had stamped a foot at one point, as if to scold herself. *You still want to go, even without understanding every little thing. Despite the danger. Because there's no better way to find Iggy, and it's that simple.*

"Does the captain owe you a favour too?" Mei asked Onolse when they reached the bottom. A different coloured stone dominated the wharves. It had a strange, clear-blue tint that gave an impression of coldness, one reinforced by armed soldiers lined up before a large guard house, which was also busy with a steady flow of people in and out.

There seemed fewer crests upon the ships and clothing here, much of which was less colourful, especially the merchants passing through in their black. Yet one noblewoman did stand out.

Golden thread was woven into her hair and the tassels on the sleeves of her pink skirts were also of a golden hue. They caught the light as she moved, her expression suggesting she had encountered something unpleasant, in contrast to the impassive faces of three soldiers that accompanied her.

These men wore breastplates engraved with images of raised swords.

At first, neither the woman's contemptuous glances nor her guards seemed to be aware of their surroundings, striding forward with barely a pause for those who were forced to make way... until Nata led her horse a little farther into the centre of the wharf.

Then the noblewoman's expression changed – a twist of anger that vanished in a flash. She stood aside, motioning for her men to do the same. They complied, scowling, but did not complain.

Nata gave them a nod. Perhaps it was meant to be of thanks, or acknowledgement, but from the flared nostrils of the noblewoman, she did not appear to appreciate the small gesture.

"Having a good time?" Mamalo asked when they turned down one of the docks that stood lined with ships, most so large that Mei had to look up to them.

"Starting to," she replied.

Mei did not ask about the exchange, for it seemed there was no particular grievance at play... or that the Greyshield even *knew* the other noblewoman. It might have been connected to some unforeseen power struggle, or perhaps Nata simply hadn't cared for the woman's unpleasant manner.

The Greyshield was a curious woman.

From a pair of empty crates by a pylon, a cat hissed at them before slinking away. Now, so close to the water itself, the pungent scent of fish and salt water filled the docks. Underfoot, scales glittered; they covered the stones and flipped and danced beneath the feet of those that walked the harbour. Here, tiny stalls had been set up along the moorings. Some were small as a single crate and a frame of fabric for shade.

As much as the towering masts and huge, cloud-like sails drew her eye, Mei also found herself staring at the merchants.

Not so refined as Mamalo or Denuko in their collars and black clothing, these men and women wore smocks or aprons;

silvery fish or coils of rope or what had to be medicines in hand as they sought attention. Some fish were so large that their spear-like noses of brilliant blue did not seem real... yet they were. So, too, the baskets filled with smooth sacs of pale pink things, some a deep crimson and yet others almost yellow.

"You eat the crimson ones because they're softer and taste almost sweet," Mamalo explained. "Tough to cut through, though."

"But not the others?"

He shook his head. "They're poisonous. But some people use them as waterproofing or to colour their paints."

"Oh."

And it was at such stalls that Senoja and Cresideth were mostly gathered, seeking fish, sacs, and salts in small cloth bags from the dock merchants, or compost courtesy of the mitiru.

Two figures were close enough to hear as they haggled with a frowning merchant. And at a glance, they could have been Inora – same fair skin and hair, blue eyes. And whether it was the bone earring or natural similarities to the language, she understood the general direction of their conversation.

Above all, the differences in language stood out.

Senoja seemed softer, seemed to have a faster rhythm too, often with different word endings that were not enough to fully obscure meaning.

But she could not stop and stare long and nor could she approach them, despite her curiosity; the others had moved on.

They'd come to a halt before a ship with two masts and a roaring creature emblazoned upon its sail. It could have been a Blood Cat, only with more hair and golden fur. Its teeth certainly looked as deadly – a lion, perhaps?

"Is your captain up to this, Nata?" Mamalo asked.

"I wouldn't trust anyone else with a task of this magnitude."

Mamalo regarded her with a raised eyebrow. "You still haven't explained exactly why you're along for this little adventure, other than to manipulate me to do the Crown's bidding, that is."

"It's more than that," she replied but did not elaborate.

"Before I risk my life – and Mei's life – I'm going to need a *much* better explanation."

Nata offered Mei a quick smile. "If you're thinking that I suspect you of being a spy, I don't, so please try not to worry." Then the Greyshield looked back to Mamalo. "Just a simple case of smuggling, Alo."

"Keep going."

"As I said, it's a case of smuggling. It could be part of something larger, but I don't know that for sure yet. That's exactly why I must investigate. You know that's how we work."

He did not seem entirely convinced. "You think they're using the Raging Isle as a staging area or a base?"

"Yes. It could explain why we haven't been able to locate their den elsewhere."

"And when you say 'they' you mean those working for or with the duke."

"I do."

"Any evidence? Any idea of what could be the larger thing? Is the duke even in the city at present?"

"Doubtful. But twice now my Eyes have reported black ships rounding the southern tip."

Mamalo shrugged. "Not enough by itself, of course."

"But enough that I must investigate."

Mei stepped between them. "Mamalo, I want to go. Will you help me?" Her decision had already been made, but at least some of his hesitation seemed to be due to concern for her. *Hopefully, this will make things go a little smoother.*

The merchant sighed. "This won't be easy. Not for a single step."

"Nothing has been, so far."

"I imagine that's true," he said as he nodded. "But I'd like to think that I have changed that somewhat."

Onolse snapped his fingers. "Perfect! Let's meet the captain."

They started up the broad, wooden ramp that led to the ship's rail, and Mei kept pace with Mamalo. "You have made a great difference, yes."

He smiled down at her. "Then I'll do my best to continue to do so."

A barefoot sailor with a blue scarf hanging down over his bare chest, approached. "Your Ladyship. Captain Minath is waiting below."

"Thank you," Nata replied as she led them across the smooth decks.

It feels quite stable. Mei glanced around the ship. A pair of sailors were working on the ropes, climbing up to long supporting beams and beneath them, a pair of barrels stood with cold lamps atop.

A ladder descended into the shadowy bowels of the ship, where Nata led them along a narrow corridor to an open door. Inside waited a stocky fellow with a big grin and white beard, the dark skin of his bald head only lightly grazed by hair. He was bellowing at his crew through a brass tube connected to the ceiling, his voice far louder than seemed possible.

Despite the power, his tone was not curt, and he laughed as he shouted.

When Nata led them into the spacious room, a place with only a bed, desk and the enormous skull of something that could not have possibly been a fish, he closed the tube. "My Lady. You are perhaps a little less punctual than promised, but welcome nonetheless."

Nata gestured to everyone. "Allow me to introduce you to those who are responsible for the delay," she said, going on to do so, but describing Mamalo as a merchant only and Mei as Senoja.

Captain Minath chuckled. "A fine answer. And an interesting party you lead."

"Best to be prepared for whatever the curse might offer us," she said.

The man nodded. "Prudent, but I've always believed the curse to be little more than a collection of stories and half-truths. Worst of it seems to be the sand-rippers. Or reefs, if you're unlucky."

"Have you been there, then?" Mamalo asked.

"I have. More by chance than design, due to a wild old storm. But if there's a fortune to be made as Lady Nata claims, then me and my crew are willing to take that risk."

"Could we discuss this further, above decks?" Onolse asked, his voice a little strained. One hand was half-raised, as if seeking a wall for balance. "I'm feeling a sudden urge for fresh air."

"We can," Captain Minath replied with a grin. "First time on a ship, is it?"

"No. This happens every time."

"And you've got no magic to help?"

The sorcerer shook his head. "I'm saving every last drop for the island."

CHAPTER 32. – MEI

Mei hung half over the railing at the front of the ship – or prow as it was called, according to Nata – staring down at the black reefs and blue water that surrounded the Raging Isle. Somehow, it was easier to keep checking on just how close Captain Minath's ship came to ruin, rather than to stare across the waves. *At least this way, I'll know when we're about to sink.*

She glanced back to where the helmsman gripped the wheel in his large hands. He wore a smile as he worked, in contrast with the rest of the sailors, it seemed.

Save for Nata and Mamalo, who were discussing something where they stood together at the opposite rail. Neither wore particularly relaxed expressions, but nor were they shouting, at least.

"Are you sure you're holding on tight?" Onolse asked. He stood nearby, gripping the rail himself. Only his gaze was fixed on the island, which was not too far distant. A dark shoreline only. For now.

"I am."

The approach had been safe enough, aside from a few scrapes. The captain had been right; reaching the Isle would not be the problem. *Which leaves the curse. If it's real.*

"Because we do need you, you know."

"Because of the spirits and their curse."

He nodded.

"And you believe they are my… ancestors? Is that why I'm supposed to be able to help?"

"The few useful reports have described words not unlike Senoja. Most of what I believe is based on a diary recovered from a shipwreck. But to know the truth, we will have to make landfall."

"If it's true, what am I supposed to say to them?"

"Explain your quest – it is a noble one, after all."

"And you think that will be enough to stop them cursing us for taking the Black Sand?"

"I hope so. If nothing else, you could attack them, yes? With your Inora gifts."

"I suppose."

"Wonderful, wonderful," he said, and fell silent then, his jaw clenched as though focusing very hard on not throwing up.

The sorcerer managed to hold on until the anchor crashed down, and again during their rockier trip to the beach upon the longboat. Relief passed over his features when they at last stood on land once more.

Mei shaded her eyes to gaze along the beach – shadowy sand as far as she could see. Only occasionally did a grey or white shell interrupt the black, and nearby, a line of clawprints, likely from a seagull. The bird's trail led toward the dunes where spiked grasses of yellow stretched. The plants, too, were colourful. Most bore bright blossoms of purple, pink, and red. They were even shaped like stars, giving them an almost magical appearance.

Beyond waited hints of green and grey, from scattered plants and shrubs that clung to stony hills. And while it did not seem the green covered everything, the colour seemed awfully vivid, even from a distance.

Captain Minath tossed his buckets down. "There is supposed to be a mountain and a lake as clear as crystal hidden within the dense jungle," he said. "Old timers claim it's that mountain that once erupted with liquid fire and made all this Black Sand."

Onolse nodded. "That is precisely what happened."

"Then, could it happen again?" Mei asked.

"It was a very long time ago," the sorcerer replied. He wiped sweat from his brow. "I'm sure we'll know if it's going to happen again. Smoke, the earth shaking and such. Things of that nature."

"What about the sand-rippers?"

The captain chuckled as he patted the huge cleaver swinging at his side. "Delicious, if you can catch them to cook. And they're easy enough to spot; they tend to go for you if you're alone. So, stick near someone and you'll be fine."

Mamalo stared across the dunes with arms folded. "Either way, let's make this quick."

The captain waved for his men to begin. They set to work dragging the buckets through the Black Sand, sloshing back through the shallows to load them into the twin longboats.

"How much is too much?" Mei asked. "Could the boats sink when we return?"

"The captain knows his work, I'm sure," Onolse said as he knelt and dug into the beach, scooping a few handfuls of

Black Sand into a pouch. "Will you keep watch for anything out of the ordinary?"

"Of course," Mei replied.

She started up the beach toward the dunes, keeping fairly close to Nata, though once she reached the top of the first, Mei hesitated. *Am I watching over the* beach *or the rest of the island?* If something terrible was going to attack, from where would it strike? Sand-rippers on the beach? But what about the curse?

Mei let her senses expand over the sand and into the dunes, as far as she could manage, but found nothing amiss. *Maybe we'll actually succeed. And quite easily.*

Below, everyone was collecting Black Sand and beside her, even Lady Nata had placed some into her purse.

"Is it truly so valuable?" Mei asked when the woman finished.

Nata nodded. "Yes. And not just to those who would trade in it or use it for magical purposes. My superiors, and thus the Royal Family, are very interested in this sand. It is even claimed the ancient peoples of Santimalu used this for astonishing feats."

"I see."

The woman smiled. "And what about you?"

Mei shook her head as she glanced down the dunes to where the coast curved around a jutting stretch of sand and out of sight. The waves crashed white against the shadows of the reef. "I'm sure Mamalo and Onolse will take enough."

"You're looking for your brother, aren't you?"

"I am, yes," Mei said, but did not add anything more. Nata didn't seem to be untrustworthy precisely, but nor did she seem like a true ally either. "What about you? Do you see any signs of the duke?"

"None, unfortunately." Nata said no more, simply stared toward the mass of bright green with a frown. It did not seem she was bothered by Mei's unwillingness to elaborate about Iggy, but that she had found nothing upon the beach.

"Have you known Mamalo a long time?" Mei asked into the silence.

"I have," the woman replied.

"Then, do you know why he is no longer a Greyshield?"

Nata exhaled. "That is a tale he might prefer to tell himself. I had not long finished training; I actually don't know all the details. But I do not believe he would find it a breach of his confidence if I offered this: he no longer believes the kingdom serves its people."

Mei stared down to where Mamalo watched the others collecting Sand. Some of the sailors seemed even a little giddy, scooping handfuls with exaggerated movements. Mamalo watched even as he paced, a sense of impatience clear even from a distance.

A kingdom that served its people? Wasn't that what the Paragons had said about Nokema when they cast Iggy out? *Even mother had claimed the same thing.* A fine reason but the cruelty of their method could not stand.

Because it was obvious they had not tried everything they could to help Iggy.

Not at all.

But I will.

Captain Minath waved from the water's edge. "That should be more than enough. Let's head home."

"Off we go then," Nata said with a shrug.

"Is something wrong?" Mei asked as she followed, feet sliding into the dark sand with each step.

"To be honest, I thought this would be difficult but the reef seems to have been the worst of it. That, and I expected to find something more here."

Mei glanced over her shoulder as the others waded into the water. The beach was silent and the dunes too... Was there even a curse? Better not to question such rare, good fortune.

***

Such unusual luck held in the longboats, which neither sank nor were attacked, and with Minath's ship too, which was able to navigate the dark reefs once again. All the while, Mei did her best to keep out from underfoot, staring across the increasingly jagged waves, unable to shake off a spectre of doubt. *How did we leave so easily? Aside from the reef, and the rumours... can I really trust our success?*

When the green line of the coast came into view, Onolse had joined her with a faint smile upon his face. He leant almost half his body across the rail. "Finally," he said.

"Are you feeling better?" Mei asked.

"Somewhat. But I am *very* keen to return home. There are several matters I must attend to. One more pressing than the others."

"The mirror?"

He nodded, but had there been just a hint of hesitation first? The sorcerer patted one of the pouches on his belt – something that also bore stitched designs of Black Coral. "With even this small amount, it will be no problem. My share will enable me to achieve much that was previously impossible."

"How long will it take?"

He grinned. "Eager, aren't we? But then, I suppose I would be too if it were my family lost in a strange land."

"I am."

"Well, since I've never made one before, I won't be rushing anything." He tapped a finger against his lips. "But if you visit tomorrow evening, everything should be ready."

"We'll be there."

CHAPTER 33. – MEI

The sunset was closer to pink than orange, spilling across the sky and its wispy clouds. Across the calm of the harbour too, as Mamalo and Nata led Mei toward Onolse's shop. Mei glanced at the ships sailing in and out as the trio strode along, and there was the *Maid of the Ocean*, where Minath and his crew were probably still celebrating.

Their cheer had been welcome, and even Mamalo seemed happy with his portion of the mysterious Black Sand, no longer frowning at everything in his path. Yet a vague doubt continued to niggle at Mei.

All she had to show for it, however, was overhearing Mamalo complain to Nata about the heat. "Am I the only one sweating so much?" he'd asked.

The Greyshield had only spread her hands. "I would have thought you'd be familiar with summer's approach by now."

At Onolse's shop, Mamalo rapped his knuckles against wood.

A moment passed and then the door swung open to reveal an old man in sorcerer's robes, his white beard and bald head both gleaming in the lamplight from within. He did not smile, but his words were pleasant enough. "How can I help you this evening?"

"We came to see Sorcerer Onolse," Mamalo said. "He is preparing an item for us and expected it to be completed today."

The old man raised an eyebrow. "Did I, now?"

Mei nearly repeated the request but could not speak at first. Had the old man said *I*? Not 'he'? That didn't make sense.

"Forgive me," Mamalo replied. "But I think there is some confusion."

Now the sorcerer smiled, though it was brief. "Perhaps. Tell me, Merchant, is the young lady here by chance named Mei?"

"She is."

"Very good. Please join me and I will explain – I believe you have been deceived."

Mei reached out but stopped short of grabbing the man. "Wait, what do you mean by that?"

"It will become clear very soon." He strode inside, leaving the door open. "Do close up behind you."

Nothing had changed in the large room, perhaps items on the long table were more neatly arranged, but there was no sign of Onolse... but then, hadn't the old man referred to himself as such?

The sorcerer took them outside to the flower garden and into the next building, which was smaller but bore larger windows. Onolse lay sleeping upon a bed in one room, and the adjoining chamber was similar, only its bed was covered in vials and half-crumpled pieces of paper.

Their guide gestured. "Meet my Apprentice, Nilo."

After a moment of silence, Mamalo muttered a curse under his breath and Nata folded her arms, though she was smiling.

Mei clenched a hand, but her anger was dulled by confusion. Why had the sorcerer lied? Had the mirror even been made?

Can he even make it? He's just an apprentice! "What is going on?"

The older sorcerer – Onolse, as it turned out – raised a hand. "I am not so thrilled about his methods either, young lady. But he's a better man than his behaviour suggests. And whatever he did was enough to save my life, and so I am planning to forgive him, as I hope you might be able, for whatever ill he has caused."

"That's why he wanted the Black Sand? To save you?"

Onolse nodded. "It was my final gamble, sending him off while I slept the sleep of the Deep Coral."

The sleep of the Deep Coral? *Sounds ominous.*

Mamalo took up the questioning. "Then, he healed you with the Black Sand, and now he is... sleeping it off?" It seemed Mamalo was quite angry again; he wiped at sweat upon his brow, the movement sharp.

"Not quite," the sorcerer replied. Then he lifted a large wooden box from the bedside table. Dark grains fell, soft as dust, as he held it out to Mei. "When I awoke, Nilo was already abed. I have not been able to rouse him, and I fear that without more Black Sand, he will not awaken. But this was waiting for you, Mei."

She accepted the box but did not open it, instead glancing to the sleeping sorcerer – Nilo, whose chest rose and fell steadily. Sweat had dampened the hair at his temples. "The same illness that you suffered from?"

He shook his head. "No. While I understood my own malady well enough to plan ahead – unlikely as I thought a cure might be – this is unknown. I have already conducted investigations, but the truth eludes me."

"What if..." Mamalo blinked as he trailed off, knees buckling.

Nata caught him. "Alo?" The merchant rasped for air as Nata lowered him to the floor.

Mei knelt beside the merchant, gripping his hand, and when she looked across to Nata, her eyes widened. Twin beads of sweat trailed down the woman's throat, sliding free from the dark hair behind her ears.

Nata frowned. "Instead of staring at me, I think we should be trying to figure out what's wrong, don't you?"

"You're sweating too."

She reached up to touch the back of her neck, her gaze growing determined. "This… if this *is* the start of whatever's happened to Mamalo and Nilo, then I don't think it'll be long before I pass out too."

"With more Black Sand, I might be able to stop whatever it is," Onolse said, a deep frown upon his face. "Otherwise, I will do my best to keep you from needless suffering."

Nata blinked down at Mamalo, as if struggling to focus. Then she looked up. "Mei, go back to the inn and bring whatever you can find."

She hesitated. Alone?

"Even the *Maid of the Ocean*. They'll have more," the Greyshield continued. "Hurry now, you might be next."

"What about all the sand Onol – Nilo returned with?"

Onolse shook his head. "I assume he used it all on a cure for me. Or your item."

Mei rose with a shiver. There seemed no other choice. *And if Nata's right, I can't waste even a single moment.*

"I'll bring what I can." She ran from the room, through the garden and into the shop, shelves flashing by as she burst into the warm streets, well-lit and full of people. There, she pumped her arms as she charged through the crowds. She drew her share of angry looks, and even one shout when she had to leap around a woman who had suddenly stopped in the centre of the street to pick something up, but Mei called an apology without turning.

When the dark water of the harbour at last came into view, a new strength flashed through her limbs – it seemed that her feet barely touched the stones.

"Hey!"

Something caught her arm, whipping her around, and she found herself face-to-face with a guard in a red cloak and burnished breastplate. The man scowled and his breath was heavy with sour milk and… something else? She shrank back and when he spoke again, it was clear why – one tooth was turning green. "Up to no good, are you, little spy?"

Mei glared, despite a trembling to her aching arm. "Let me go."

"Not likely," he snapped. "You'll be coming with me to answer some questions."

Mei lashed out with her mind.

The guard released his grip, stumbling back. He clutched at his head but had not fallen – Mei struck again. A dent appeared in his armour, the blow hammering into the guard's stomach. He crashed down and Mei resumed her flight, boots pounding across the wharf.

She glanced over her shoulder as she ran, but no-one followed… and it seemed few had even moved to check upon the guard. Plenty of people seemed to watch her, however. *I can't stop now.*

Finally, Mei skidded to a halt before the ship. She called for Captain Minath but no-one answered, and more, the decks were empty.

Is this an ill omen?

She ran up the planks and crossed the deck, heading 'stern' as she'd heard the direction referred to, and on her way down the ladder, she came across two bodies… but not corpses.

Two sailors lay slumped against the wall, both sweating as they slept.

The same fever?

In the captain's room with its giant skull, she found him slumped over his desk, quill in hand. An ink-pot had overturned; black spread across timber.

"Captain Minath?" Even before she lifted him back into his chair, she knew he would be sweating from the same fever… the same curse?

She swallowed. *How long until I collapse too?*

Could the real Onolse save everyone? Mei found her own breath quickening as she grabbed the handle to the first drawer… locked. She frowned at it, using just enough of her power for the lock snap open.

Inside, four large pouches of Black Sand. *How many will he need?*

She snatched up two, since any more would be difficult to carry *and* defend herself from other guards, then ran from the room. "We'll be back to save you, too," she said, even though the man may not have heard.

Upon the deck, she paused to stare out across the black water, toward where the sun had set, and to where the Raging Isle would have waited. Was the island truly cursed?

There was no time to ponder.

Go, go, go!

CHAPTER 34. – CINDER

As the villagers strode from bright fields of wheat, Cinder kept to the column's rear, alongside Denuko and his wagon. Grim faces everywhere he looked. Thinking of those they left behind in the cavern?

Or what they were about to face?

And it would not be long. Halfway to the reported column of sand-stalkers, the group had come across Ketaj, the young man having collapsed against a fence to wait like a signpost at a crossroad.

Cinder reached up to touch his brow, where a relatively new scar rested. *Unpleasant memories, indeed.*

But Mikal and the others had offered the scout water and encouragement, standing around him, yet not so close as to cast a shadow. The older man even gently chastised Denuko when he bent to hand over something from the healer, and the merchant's shadow fell across Ketaj.

Denuko had nodded, stepping aside in a timely fashion.

When the full extent of the sun fell upon Ketaj once more, the young fellow seemed to sigh in relief.

Curious.

The scout was soon strong enough to speak again, and after his explanation, whatever it was, the score of villagers continued on with perhaps a new determination. Ketaj seemed well enough also, walking up front with Mikal and Galarik.

And now, at last, while the sun still shone, they had stopped to form a line and wait.

Cinder moved back.

But there was nothing upon the road ahead, just swaying grasses of a plain; parts quite yellow, yet with enough wildflowers for little black butterflies to flit about. The rising wind tugged at his clothes and he sighed.

"Regretting your choice?" Denuko asked as he started back toward the wagon, where he began shuffling the modest amount of supplies around. Supposedly, to make room for the wounded or exhausted, depending on what happened.

Cinder joined him. "Yes."

"No need to feel that way." The man moved to check on his horses next. "It's the right choice, and besides which, I think we're about to see something remarkable. Maybe remarkable enough to save Nokema."

"We are?"

"Yes. Paragon Mikal will lead them in joining their gifts to strike down the *arkedi*."

Such a claim was... unclear, but based on the scores of shimmering figures that were now rising from the plain ahead, it would happen soon enough.

Each creature was only vaguely human-shaped. And despite their relative distance, it was impossible to miss specks of sand falling to the earth with each movement. Every single grain a deadly poison too. Nevertheless, there was something alluring about the shapes… Cinder stepped forward, then stopped with a shudder.

The Inora were less enamoured of the creatures.

Mikal had extended his hands to those on either side, as had the rest of the villagers, jaws set or shoulders tensed. The air grew very still. And though the *arkedi* were drawing close now, their narrow faces bearing gaping mouths, the Inora had not struck.

"What are they waiting for?" he asked Denuko.

"I don't know. But we shouldn't stand too close." He gave some more ground, and Cinder joined him, reaching for the hilt of the stolen blade. Would such a thing be of any use if the Inora failed?

Not that I plan to find out.

A shout echoed across the plain – Mikal's voice.

Upon the heels of his cry, *something* tore the grass as it burst from the line of villagers.

The horde of sand-stalkers shattered.

Countless sparkling grains spread in the air, floating far and wide. Cinder fell back; such power! And all in barely a moment, without a sound. Just how dangerous were the Inora, really?

But the strike was not without a cost, as the breeze had caught enough pieces of the *arkedi* to drift toward the line of Inora.

So few were still standing, others struggling to catch their breath.

Denuko had already dashed forward, pulling people to their feet. Cinder groaned. The wind wasn't so strong that he'd be at risk if he joined in… hopefully. He ran to a woman with grey-streaked hair tied into a bun, lifting her up. "Quickly," he said as she stumbled toward the wagon.

The merchant had already collected another villager, the sparkling sand swooping closer… some of the Inora were crawling toward safety now. *This is getting worse.* Cinder muttered a curse now, leaping back to the line to assist someone else, then another, soon breathing hard himself.

But between himself and Denuko, and the Inora who could still stand, it seemed to be enough where they gathered by the merchant's wagon.

Mikal was checking on the woman Cinder helped, and upon seeing that she was well enough, he smiled at her before moving to Galarik. The two conferred for but a short time, then called for Denuko.

While both men wore expressions of weary relief, they had not truly relaxed; Mikal in particular was showing signs of fatigue in the way that he blinked. His legs even trembled a little, despite the man seeming to do his best to conceal the strain.

Cinder moved a little closer. The merchant was nodding along at whatever was being said, and then he glanced around. "Cinder? The Paragons have a request."

"For me?"

Denuko nodded. "It is dangerous. I would do it, but I need to help get them back to the cavern. Will you go in my place?"

"Where?"

"To ensure that there are no more of them approaching from the fissure."

Cinder affected a pause of doubt. *Finally, my chance to escape.* "If it is only to check, I can do that."

"Good. Unhitch Flip and take her," Denuko said. "Just make sure you return by dark, to be safe."

Cinder nodded.

Mikal was smiling across at him. "Thank you. May the sun guide you."

Gratitude even shone in Galarik's eyes, and Cinder had to move to the wagon without answer.

CHAPTER 35. – ANYO

Anyo rode through the gentle hills at a trot beside Femithir Nuvin, keeping Han and Katonga within sight. Ahead, their new mounts crossed a small stone bridge that spanned trickling streams of pure blue. Elin and Fiana were speaking softly with Binya to the rear; it seemed Binya was explaining how she came to join the quest for the Mirror Blade.

Beside him, Nuvin turned toward the grassy plains and the distant shape of Dibora. He raised a hand, palm upward, and a robin of brown and red feathers fluttered down, chirped a moment before flying away just as swiftly.

"Thank you, friend," Nuvin said.

"What of the road ahead?" Anyo asked, staring after the bird. *Aehtu, that's still a little hard to believe.*

"Nothing amiss, for now. A pair of hunters in a wood to the west, an abandoned farm ahead – generations of poor soil for vegetables, rather than something to trouble us."

"Generations of poor soil? The birds know that much?"

He smiled. "Owls especially, but most animals know the histories of their homes. It is passed down through the generations."

"Do you mean they share memories?"

"Not precisely. It is more that they become attuned to a place over generations. They can read what has occurred in the lands where they make their home; their instincts are fed by not only the present and their more sophisticated senses, but their history. Of course, my father claimed it was we Femithir who draw out events and memories *from* the animals, especially birds, those who see so much."

"Then... it isn't language. You cannot understand birds chirping."

"No, not like that."

Anyo met the man's calm gaze. "Perhaps you really can help us find the Sothalic."

"Oh? You doubted me before now?"

"Yes. Your knowledge is obviously of extreme value, and the horses and the extra blades are welcome, should we run into more conventional difficulties, but I hadn't really understood about your gifts," Anyo said, as he explained the two possible paths for their search. "If birds or other animals witnessed the descendant or the songbird herself, or simply felt the power of the Sothalic's passage at all, we have a real chance to narrow things down."

"That we do."

By nightfall, they set up camp within sight of the road and once more, Nuvin and his sisters offered to share the sweet drink from their homeland but only Binya and Katonga accepted the offer.

Han kept to his cooking and Anyo found himself repairing two significant tears in his cloak, working steadily rather than swiftly with needle and thread, counting the stitches as he did.

They would soon reach the mountains and the border… which would mean sneaking or breaking through, but was it possible considering just how large – and attentive – the garrison would be?

"Something troubling you?" Nuvin asked. "Perhaps the border?"

Anyo looked west to where the shadowy mountains lurked. "The border is farther into the mountains than our first hurdle, I suppose – the Gabokam garrison."

"I see. Our travel within these lands is somewhat limited."

"The garrison is two-thousand strong, which is not counting the townspeople who would share the same suspicions as the king's forces. We would draw unwanted attention, even if I were not… infamous."

"And there are no other trails we could use to traverse the pass?"

"None that I can recall. That is why the garrison is placed where it is." He glanced at Han. "Any ideas?"

The man paused where he was dishing out bowls of stew with a sigh. "It's nothing we'd planned for to begin with, heading this far west."

"Yet here we are," Anyo said.

"Aye. There may be other, older paths but I do not know them either."

"I will ask the birds, if needed," Nuvin offered.

"What about a diversion?" one of Nuvin's sisters asked. Elin, whose dark hair was short, unlike her sister's.

Katonga nodded. "It would have to be big, to let us sneak through. No idea what we could use, though… to distract that many troops would probably mean something terrible enough to endanger ourselves."

"Bluffing?" Binya asked. "Think you could fool them into

believing you're one of your brothers, Anyo?"

Anyo rubbed at his cheek. "Balo, perhaps. If the guards we encountered were younger than average… But it would also depend on the commander at Gabokam. Obviously, the nobility especially, are all quite familiar with my family."

Katonga frowned into the flames.

Nuvin and his sisters were equally silent.

Then the Femithir spoke. "As offered, I can scout the town and troop positions via the birds or other animals, so you can have all the specific information you need about sentry movements or numbers or perhaps even older secrets, but we will not know until we draw nearer."

"That would be useful, whatever we choose," Anyo replied. "Yet I suspect we cannot risk any of those options, considering just how suspicious we will appear."

Han snorted. "Not to mention how much a good deal of your family would love to clap you in irons."

"Exactly."

"Then where does that leave us?" Binya asked between mouthfuls, her cheeks becoming almost comically large in the firelight.

"In need of something else," Anyo said.

Nuvin tapped his fingers against his knee. "I suspect any path circling the Senkaisem Ranges will take us some weeks or even months out of our way?"

"Yes," Anyo replied. "On top of which, those highways will be watched closely by the nobility and the Senoja themselves. We would need to seek more clandestine roads."

Nuvin frowned. "Such a delay could prove disastrous, should the Moon Father awaken before we locate the sword."

Again, another bout of quiet with only the warm crackle of flames.

Katonga stood and began to pace, shifting in and out of the firelight, an orange glow moving across his fine features. "If we cannot go over or around, what about *under* the mountain?"

Anyo straightened as a memory struck. "Perhaps there *is* one other path."

"Being?" Binya asked.

"Once, I overheard Father and Mother speaking with their generals. I had hidden myself beneath the banquet table, just to be near," he said with a smile. "At first, I was content to play with my wooden soldiers but when their voices changed, the tension cut through to me. As the silences grew longer, I paid more attention."

"That is quite the picture," Binya said with her own smile.

He chuckled. "Of a somewhat needy child, I admit. But somehow, it's a fond memory, despite their words. Father was not so… driven, back then."

"What words?" Nuvin asked.

"The generals were speaking of a disused network of… flying carriages, supposedly strung upon mighty steel cables. The way they were described, it sounded as though these carriages could carry people across the range."

Binya raised an eyebrow. "Flying carriages?"

"I know. It sounds unlikely. And I don't know if it is an exaggeration of either my memory or the generals themselves, but what they described probably seemed as much. Riding the carriages with treetops and gorges below, sliding from peak to peak on such cables. Sky Carriages."

"No, I actually know the path of which you speak," Han

said with a solemn nod. "And your memory is not faulty. But it was abandoned for a good reason."

"Why?" Binya had leant forward, as had everyone else. Katonga, too, was no longer pacing.

"What more do you know, lad?" Han asked.

"I remember little else. Only that the generals wanted to use them to send assassins. I do not remember who the target was supposed to be, nor why the Sky Carriages were not actually used."

"As to who, that is no longer important," Han said. "But the carriages were constructed at great cost, over decades, by peoples of this land in the years before the unification. Or so your father's Royal Sorcerers eventually discovered."

"I see. And the problem was... their age?"

"Well, two problems came to light. The scouting party – or I should say, clearing party – eventually reached a stone gate that could not be opened. This was perhaps halfway to the pass that led down into Senoja, by their estimation."

"Hmmm." If a group of Royal Coral Sorcerers could not pass... "And the second thing?"

"Is whatever killed most of them on the way back. There were three survivors from a force of two score," Han replied. "The full reports are stored somewhere in the palace, but I was not privy to such things."

"You didn't speak to the survivors?"

Han shook his head. "Supposedly, few had the chance. It was said that one never left their room again. The second survivor threw themselves from one of towers years later. The third died from their wounds not long after returning. Against something like that, I do not believe we could survive."

Anyo exhaled heavily. Did that leave only a detour, after all? Or an attempt at bluffing? "Very well. The Sky Carriages do not seem a viable choice, but before we try anything, we will need information. Nuvin, what can the animals tell us about the camp?"

He rose. "Let me start with some birds and see what can be discovered."

"Wait," Binya said. "Won't the birds know about the flying carriages too?"

"Doubtless."

"Is that worth investigating?" Anyo asked.

"It might be," Binya replied. "At least, *if* the descendant or Misha herself used them."

Katonga shrugged as he took his seat once more. "Suppose she lost the Sothalic during her flight somehow, and it's just sitting there beneath the cable's path? We wouldn't ever know."

"Well, I wasn't suggesting something like that precisely," Binya said.

"Either way, we need information before we take another step." Anyo stared across the darkened plain below, to the small glow of the border garrison's camp.

CHAPTER 36. – ANYO

By morning, still they had not shifted from their vantage point, had not made any move either toward the camp, nor away from the border, not in any direction. Ever since the return of the last of Nuvin's birds at daybreak, Anyo had not been able to shake the sense that fate was playing a cruel joke upon him.

It had taken time for the Femithir to fully describe the camp, the troops and their movements, translating from the impressions of four different birds and one soft-furred deer that approached but kept her distance. But when Anyo asked about the commander, the answer had him shaking his head with a bitter smile.

"What's funny?" Binya had asked.

"The two wings and blade upon the Royal Standard. It's my brother. Ebatru is in command of the garrison. Of all the places!"

Han exhaled heavily, but Katonga grinned. "Well, you do have six siblings and there is fresh tension with Senoja. It's not so outlandish for your father to send someone he trusts out here."

"As true as that likely is," Anyo had replied, "I think it leaves us with two options. Distraction or detour."

And now he found himself taking up Katonga's pacing from last night, counting his steps, as if the action of walking across the loam would somehow trigger a solution or even a new idea.

Fruitless, of course.

Worse, if Nuvin's birds could not find a path that skirted the garrison and then in turn, the actual border, a long detour would have to be taken after all. Any delay would not be a problem for finding the songstress or the Sothalic, but the pale walkers? The so-called Moon Children?

Are they actually after me *because I'm searching for the Mirror Blade?*

He sighed. The quest for the blade, and his honour, had grown into something incredibly vast. Even before Nuvin's story of the Moon Father threatening the world, wanting to change the city *and* the nation was an enormous undertaking. *And now, I have an invisible deadline to beat.*

"We need to leave."

Han's voice broke through and Anyo spun to face the garrison. Horses were rallying forth, based on the clouds of dust.

"How do they know we're here?" Katonga asked. "*Do* they know we're here?"

"Sorcerers, I'd guess," Han replied. "It's possible they're just scouting the area, but I don't want to risk sticking around either way, do you?"

"Not for a moment."

"Break camp," Anyo ordered, and set to work stuffing his bedding into his saddlebags. "We can keep ahead of them easily enough."

"But to where?" Binya asked.

Anyo swore. "We could turn back, hide in Dibora."

"The sorcerers might make that harder," Han said. "If they pick up our trail – supposing they haven't already, which seems unlikely."

"Nuvin?" Anyo turned to the man with more than a little hope.

"Little I can do with my gifts, sadly." He was already packed and was helping his sisters restring their bows, movements deft. "You have my spear, but we're going to be outnumbered."

"Of course." He glanced up at the peaks, the rising sun turning the stone from black to grey. "Into the mountains then."

Katonga raised an eyebrow as he finished mounting up. "You don't mean –"

"A last resort; we just need to find a good hiding place to throw them off our scent. Sorcerers or no, we have to try something."

"Better than staying here," Binya said, and kicked her own mare into a trot, heading up the stony trail.

"Can you guide us, Nuvin?" Han asked.

"Of course."

And then they were moving along the trail, passing tumbled stone and strewn needles from rows of pine. The trail wound in and out of shade with few detours, and those they did pass were not worth investigating.

Once, Anyo noted a few figures carved into a greying trunk – rabbit, deer and bear.

A message for hunters, no doubt. And one that travellers ought to take note of also – especially the bear. *Which might just rule out using a cave as a hiding place…*

By late morning, Nuvin halted at a fork in the trail.

"Doesn't sound like they've given up," Katonga called from the rear. "In fact, they've gained on us."

"How?" Binya asked.

Anyo was frowning at the two paths ahead, though neither seemed all that different. "Ebatru is probably using the Coral as a stimulant for the horses. And maybe his men, too. It's an old military trick."

"Isn't that dangerous?"

Nuvin glanced over his shoulder. "I have heard of such a thing. How long can it be used?"

"A day at the most."

He frowned. "Then we are not going to be able to outrun them, after all."

"But can we conceal ourselves somewhere?"

"Perhaps." Nuvin pointed to the right. "The birds assure me there are several candidates for suitable hiding places, but I am not certain we will reach them in time. Nor that we can remain hidden, if the sorcerers have found a way to locate us to begin with."

"And the left?" Anyo asked.

"Will lead to a passage that takes us to the Sky Carriages."

Katonga groaned. "We don't have a choice do we?"

Silence filled the crossroads until a new bird fluttered down to chirp from where it landed upon Nuvin's hand. "The tunnel that will lead us to the Sky Carriages is clear."

All eyes turned to Anyo.

He dismounted. "Bring whatever you can carry. Nuvin, tell the horses to take the right fork. We're going to the Sky

Carriages. Even if our ploy doesn't end up buying us much time, my brother won't follow."

Han exhaled. "You're assuming he knows about the danger and won't follow, aren't you?"

He nodded. "You knew, so why not Ebatru? After all, he has taken responsibility for guarding the border. He'd have to be aware of the carriages."

"Sound reasoning," Nuvin added.

Binya was frowning but offered no objection. The sisters appeared calm enough, simply waiting for Nuvin to move, it seemed.

Finally, Katonga chuckled. "Just like I feared. But we really are out of options, aren't we?"

"I believe so." Anyo collected his pack and patted his horse's neck before starting up the left fork, footfalls ringing in the quiet. And it did not take long for the others to follow; their trust lent strength to his steps but would it be enough?

The longer they walked, the more overgrown the trail became.

"It won't be difficult to mark our passage," Han grumbled.

"Sadly."

They came across the opening – a great, jagged wound cut into the very rock face and flanked by an old landslide on one side. Piles of pine needles covered the earth, and Anyo stopped to light a lamp.

Then he glanced back at everyone, took his first steps within.

Dark and cool, the ground was uneven and covered in dust and more old needles. Lace-like webs adorned the space but caused no real barrier to his movement. How long was it? And what exactly waited on the other side? On they walked, and when he reached the point where natural light beckoned, it revealed only a funnel-like forest trail where darkened trees climbed up beneath more stretching stone walls.

Outside, Anyo paused to check upon the others. "Be watchful, everyone."

Binya and the Cresi murmured their affirmative responses, as did the others, save for Han who only nodded. His eyes revealed some strain, but he soon straightened. Anyo could not prevent a frown. *Is he hiding how hard this has become on him?*

Thankfully, Han didn't notice the frown of concern. It most definitely would have hurt his pride. Anyo approached the trail; another overgrown path with barely a few patches of clear earth. Bark seemed to be peeling from every trunk.

A hush filled the trail too. The absence of expected sounds from birds or animals moving through undergrowth was all the more unusual after having so many hovering around Nuvin.

Anyo split his attention between the trees and the trail ahead. Binya walked beside him, and it seemed as though she was about to speak, though she did not offer anything at first. She was almost glaring at the trees with their trailing bark, some of which appeared like pine but with brighter needles. Other dark colours stretched up in thin lines, their tops mostly hidden as they slipped through the canopy.

Orange and purple blossoms, shaped almost as spirals, lay at the foot of these trees, sometimes spilling into others or falling across the path.

"Anyo, I would ask you something." Binya had not taken her eyes from the trail, her voice kept low.

"Yes?" Whether it was the tales about the place, Han's reaction or the hush, Anyo too, did not look her way for very long. Far safer, it seemed, to focus on the unseen threat that supposedly lurked within the mountain.

"I believe you know that I am not one to hold my tongue."

He almost smiled. "You are not."

"Good. Then my question is simply this, what do you intend to do, should you succeed in finding the Sothalic?"

"You know the answer to that question."

"I know what you *desire*. That doesn't mean you will go through with it," she said. "And that's what I am trying to measure, since I am risking my life more and more often, and in increasingly dire situations, while I travel with you."

He frowned. "Are you asking for a higher payment?"

"Yes." She moved a little closer. "But money is not going to be enough."

Now he stopped, his own voice dropping almost to a hiss. "What more can I offer?"

"Your oath, of course."

"I already pledged to as much, pledged to make the lives of Takirov better – and I meant those words."

"I am talking about the new threat. The so-called Moon Father."

"We will face that also."

"That's not what I am asking, Your Highness. I want your oath to my people to come before whatever happens with those creatures. Defeat them when they stand in your way, yes, but changing Nasaru must happen before the concerns of the Cresideth."

He folded his arms. "I did not make an oath to your people. And I do not believe you are so single-minded that you cannot see that the Pale Walkers are a threat to all."

"Of course." Binya's expression hardened. "But my

responsibility is clear; I am no coward who would fail to fight for my people. I have a chance that no other woman of Takirov has been given – and by luck or design it is here, and I dare not waste it. I plan to take any and every chance to influence you, the only one who has promised to make change. *You* are fighting for what you believe is right when you seek the Sothalic, when you dream of deposing your corrupted family. I am the same when I dream of a better future for my people." She looked at him then. "I am the same."

Anyo had kept a handle on a rising anger at her words, something of their callous truth cutting deeper than mere outrage at her audacity. *She is hardly wrong about our similarities.* "If that were true, you would not ask me to put *your* concerns above something that could threaten each and every land, not merely our own."

"I will leave the world to you, Prince Anyo – all *I* need do is hold you to your promise. That is my oath to my people. Live up to the ideals I know you hold. Honour your word."

"Enough." Anyo strode ahead. "I have not once said I will ignore the suffering in my own nation."

"And if we survive this place, know that I will remind you of that," Binya replied.

CHAPTER 37. – ANYO

Sky Carriages certainly were no myth.

The overgrown trail had ended, replaced by a wide clearing. A gorge lurked beyond, but a towering structure of black steel dominated the place. It surged up from the stony earth in pillars thick enough to rival tree trunks. The pillars did not surround a building either – they were the structure itself, supporting mighty steel cables hung with large carriages that stretched off into the mountain, rising like the arc of an arrow.

Anyo could not trace the end point; it disappeared beyond the first peak. *Not so dissimilar to what can be found in the City of Rope, in a way.*

Compelling as the structure was, something else seemed to be keeping everyone at the edge of the tree line.

Something that, at first, Anyo had not been able to fathom.

Stacks of timber, faded to grey, crossed in neat lines. Only three stacks sat within the open space, in no particular arrangement and only chest high, but when he spotted what seemed to be feet… and faces… the word 'only' was no longer appropriate.

"What horror is this?" Nuvin asked, the first to move into the clearing.

His sisters flanked him, arrows held to bowstrings.

Anyo drew his own blade as he followed to examine the stacks… emaciated bodies placed like lumber, caught forever in decay, limbs stiffened and leeched of most colour. From what remained of their garments, they seemed Nasaru in design.

Whatever the case, their clothing had been pressed against skin, almost as if the victims had been doused in water before being frozen in place.

How were they preserved? *No, instead – who or* what *would do such a thing in the first place?*

"Do your birds have anything to say about this atrocity?" Han asked Nuvin.

The Femithir frowned up at the sky. "I have called, but they are hesitant to come here. They consider it a dread place, that much we already know, however."

"What of the pillars, then?" Katonga asked after a moment's silence. "Might as well see if we can actually use the carriages."

Anyo nodded. "Han, watch with him. Elina and Fiana, would you please scout the area?"

The sisters nodded and started a circuit of the clearing, heading for the trees.

Up close, the pillars did seem to be steel, but the black colour was not so even – it was a rigid pattern, like interlocking squares and rectangles. He reached out and his fingertips trailed over faint grooves. Flipping a dagger into his hand, he tapped the pommel against the surface and a faint, bell-like chime filled the clearing.

"How did the Old Ones make this?" Binya asked from beside him.

He shrugged as he circled, stopping before the opening.

Inside, two spacious carriages hung from the bulky cables, which fed into a huge cogwheel. The carriages themselves were constructed from the same unusual steel, and though it was obviously thinner than the columns that housed the cog, would they truly be any weaker for it? Each carriage bore sturdy-looking glass too, with a carved handle upon the door.

Anyo turned the handle; it opened on silent hinges to reveal seats lined with fur, and room enough for four. In the centre of the carriage, accessible to any riding within, rested a column bearing a dark lever, inlaid with bronze.

He leant in and put pressure on the lever.

It clicked into a forward position, but nothing happened.

"They must need something else to move," Nuvin said from the other side of the carriage, his voice muffled somewhat by the layers of glass.

"What about this?" Binya asked. She stood to the rear, looking down on what seemed to be a small opening in the wall; a smooth steel hatch. Its little window appeared bronze in colour, if not finish. "Maybe it needs something placed inside to lend it power… to make it move. It almost seems to be a hearth, for a fire."

"What makes you say that?" Nuvin said as he approached.

Anyo joined them. There *was* room enough for something to rest within, wood or perhaps a bed of coal, but how would fire make the carriages move? Better to have a team of horses—or oxen—to turn the wheel. "We need to find something. This might not be what we need, but there isn't much else around."

From the outside, Elin and Fiana called for everyone to gather.

They stood before a heap of glass vials at the edge of the

clearing, joined by Katonga, who stared down with blade still in hand. Han had not joined them, instead he glared across the gorge. When Anyo followed his gaze, there was naught but treetops and mountain peaks.

The vials were filled with what could have been sand… only, it was black. Anyo lifted one; it was surprisingly heavy. Was it actually something more than sand?

"We found many more vials scattered amongst the trees," Elin said.

"Most had been smashed open, some covered in a grey film," Fiana added. "There were at least five times as many as what we brought back."

Anyo glanced back to the stacks of bodies. "I don't believe they would have done such a thing."

"Let's fill the chamber within," Nuvin suggested.

"It doesn't appear to be coral, if that's what you're thinking," Katonga replied.

"But we should try it anyway, right?"

Katonga nodded.

Anyo lifted four vials, at least a third of what the sisters had gathered, and returned to the hatch and its window. "If this does make the carriage move, we'll take the rest with us just in case." He unstoppered the vial and poured the first one down the hatch, filling it a third of the way. A sharp scent rose from the vial, enough to sting his airways. Two more and then it was full, the strange black sand settling softly.

Yet as before, nothing changed.

"Try the lever now," Nuvin said. Anyo moved to the nearer carriage and reached inside to push the black and bronze lever. It slid into place and *something* seemed to hum through the carriage, along the cable and back toward the hatch.

He glanced over his shoulder. The black sand began to shift, swirling in place, becoming a tiny whirlwind. Yet the force within did not cause the hatch itself to so much as even tremble.

However, the Sky Carriage lurched forward.

Anyo snatched at the lever, bringing it back to a neutral position, halting the carriage. He smiled. "That answers that."

A new voice spoke from beyond the pillars. "That answers what, exactly?"

Anyo circled the carriage.

There, flanked by soldiers in red cloaks pouring into the clearing, and aided by no less than six Coral Sorcerers – the wall of flesh and muscle that was his brother, Ebatru.

CHAPTER 38. – ROKURA

Sunlight poured through the large hole Iggy had blasted in the trunk, revealing more ash spread across dark earth. Inside, the ash was not so concentrated, uneven piles leading into shadows that lurked beyond the limit of the illumination.

No hints of movement reached Rokura. Barely even a puffing sound when a large splinter fell from the opening either.

"That certainly opened a path," he said as he drew two blades and stepped inside.

Let me lead. I can probably see better in there.

"True, but if I cannot see you, we'll still have trouble," he replied as he slung his pack free and knelt. "Let me get the lamp."

Once they had light, Rokura lifted it and followed Iggy.

High above, tiny points of sunlight slid down, hardly enough to make much difference. The lamp soon became the only meaningful source of illumination, with the opening so far behind. Here, the earth beneath his feet had grown far smoother, free of ash, but it wasn't until his boot gave a squeak that it became clear just how smooth the ground had become.

Not dirt at all.

Not *ground* at all; but a surface more akin to flooring.

"A moment, Iggy." Rokura knelt and ran a hand across a dark, gleaming floor – not unlike tiles, yet he found no seam, no hint that it had been joined. "More mysteries," he muttered as he rose and continued on, explaining to Iggy, who only nodded.

It soon became apparent that the duration of the walk seemed more than the trunk could contain. But despite the dark and unnatural span, despite the smooth floor that ought not have existed, a distinct lack of danger filled the place. But why? No sense that something monstrous was lying in wait. Nuka had claimed the Mistress would welcome them, or at least be curious... but what if she was instead cloaking her ill intent? If twenty Coral Sorcerers could not face her, was even Iggy's unusual power enough?

We won't know until we meet her.

Rokura sighed. "Is it always that easy to read my mind?'

Not always. The thoughts that cry out with their urgency are easiest to pluck.

"Low-hanging fruit, I suppose."

Very much so.

On they walked, until Iggy slowed at the faint echo of some gentle, stringed instrument, unseen…

"Welcome to you both." A dark, rich voice echoed within the shadows, soothing and calm – no trace of fury or threat within her words.

The inky black swirled, parted by an enormous flower of deep purple, whose spiral petals glowed. Rokura straightened as a giant leg slid free of the petals, smooth skin glimpsed beneath a lattice of glimmering fabric that could have been web, could have been silver. Her torso and smiling face followed, dark lips and bright eyes half-concealed by long curls. Even her hair seemed aglow where it swayed, still settling long after she leant down from where she towered over them both.

The Mistress of Obsidian.

She was most definitely real.

Rokura gripped his blade, though his safety – his life – rested in Iggy's hands now.

Nuka said you might be the only one that can help me, Mistress.

"That might be true." She settled back into the flower and crossed her legs; the petals supported her like a soft armchair, a perfumed throne. From her voice, her posture, her smile, everything seemed safe enough.

At least, for now. At least, if her whole manner of calmness was no ruse.

"You seek acceptance, Iggy of Nokema."

I came to ask if you can give me a face.

"That is hardly a guarantee of acceptance."

I am small but I am not a child. His reply was curt. Rokura tensed, but the Mistress only waved a hand.

"My, my. While it is true that for you, a face will change your life, I say again that you may still not find the acceptance you seek, even with something so many take for granted. At least, what if it is not possible here, in the lands beyond your Valley?"

I have to take that risk.

The Mistress smiled once more, then glanced at Rokura. "And you, Greyshield of Nasaru. What do you seek from the Mistress of Obsidian?"

Her beauty was even stronger when she gazed down at him, and his mouth grew dry. Rokura cleared his throat – her power too, seemed larger but more... considerate than Nuka, whose touch had been subtle as a war-hammer.

Even so, he could not find words to answer her at first. "Former Greyshield, Mistress. But I ask only that you grant Iggy what he seeks."

"Noble, as expected. You do not need the cloth to live the ideals, yes? I cannot wonder if you are certain of that fact, if you *feel* what your mind tells you to believe."

"I am certain."

"I see." The Mistress of Obsidian opened her palm, and upon it rested a transparent box of red velvet, an illusion. "I can indeed grant Iggy a face but in return, I expect something from you, young man."

Gladly.

"Retrieve the contents of this box for me and I will give you what you ask," she said. "That is all."

I will do it. Where does the box lie?

"Wait, Iggy," Rokura said. "We have more questions."

The Mistress of Obsidian nodded. "Ask."

"What is inside?"

"That, I cannot say. But I will add that it poses no threat to you, Rokura, Iggy or the people of this nation. Not even your sorcerers, if that is what concerns you."

"Should it concern me, Mistress?"

She gestured to the darkness. "I am bound to this place and have no desire to leave to attack the descendants of those already most justly punished. As I hope you are aware, none have died by my hand since those rabid fools came for my head."

Why did they want your head?

"Because they believed I could be used to fuel their warmongering, why else? Perhaps it might have been true, but my life does not come so cheaply, as they discovered."

Her words did not match the legends. Old stories were often twisted by time but the Mistress of Obsidian could just as easily tell a tale that suited her. Still, in some ways it did not matter since Iggy had already decided. *He'd probably already decided before reaching this place.*

"And where are we to look for this box?" Rokura asked.

"South, off the coast of Makmirdrys."

Iggy turned to Rokura. *Where is that? In Takirov?*

"Yes. Today it is known as Makmir." He looked up at the Mistress. "That is the coast we must search?"

"Upon the *Silver Shark* where it sleeps beneath the waves, yes."

Nuka said that is why you believe I can help.

"Yes. Who better to seek it out? With your gifts and your affinity for water, you have a chance where Coral Sorcerers and Takirov water-weavers have failed in the past."

Then, you've sent others before me?

"Not at all. The wreck of the *Silver Shark* has long been of interest to treasure hunters. Of course, all have failed."

But you believe I won't?

She smiled. "I let you live long enough to speak to me, didn't I?"

Iggy chuckled; the first time Rokura had even heard such a sound from the lad's mind. *That almost gives me confidence.*

"Good. Know that the Fates are expecting great things from you both," she said, settling back into the petals once more. "As you leave, you will find the path back hardly so long."

"Mistress, before we do so, will you swear an oath?" Rokura asked.

For the first time since meeting her, the woman frowned. "You ask that of me?"

"Of all whom I deal with," he said, somehow managing *not* to step back. "Would you have me doubt your honour?"

"I do not feel that would be in question. I am no human, fit to snarl and snipe and betray."

"Then I ask for the sake of my duty to protect Iggy."

She regarded him for a long moment. "Hmmm. Very well, Rokura, Former Greyshield and man of honour. I give my word that should you return with the contents of the red box, then I will grant Iggy's wish."

He lowered himself to one knee. "Thank you."

"Very well. Now, off you go, seekers. Return triumphant."

The Mistress of Obsidian began to fade, darkness swallowing the throne of petals and her smile alike.

CHAPTER 39. – ROKURA

Rokura wiped sweat from his brow as he set the last of the orange-barrels down. Once he finished, he crossed the deck to lean against the railing and rest his weary limbs to the sound of rope creaking and the sail snapping above.

The surging grey of the water, flashing beneath the noon sun, flowed swiftly below in hues that seemed fashioned by the river to torment him. The still green and yellow grass of the plains was more agreeable, as was the blue sky with its faint threads of cloud.

The closer the *River Queen* came to the coast, due to arrive by tomorrow morning, the harder it remained to stave off his doubts.

Not about the Mistress of Obsidian. After all, was staying isolated and using a terrifying reputation to keep people away even a ploy? No. Not at all the best way to lure in the unwary. But she was hardly what he had imagined, not precisely what the legends had suggested either. Yet could she truly deliver on her promise?

Was she actually bound to that place?

So much depended on whether she and Nuka would keep

their word. *Assuming Iggy can find the mysterious box.*

"All done, then?" The first mate approached and handed over a small pouch of coin, his broad face and greying beard split by a smile. "I've been meaning to ask, what business do you and your sickly friend have in Makmir?"

"Gambling, actually," Rokura replied as he thanked the man. Getting information about the wreck of the *Silver Shark*, something he had only a bare familiarity with, would be easier with a story that suited appearances. After all, plenty were those who set out from their home seeking fortune. "Like many before me, I'm sure, I'm seeking the treasure of the *Silver Shark*."

The sailor chuckled. "Ah, I see what you mean by gambling. That's a desperate, final toss of the dice, there."

Rokura nodded. "While I still can, you see. The years are turning a little too fast for my liking."

The man nodded. "Aye, I understand that feeling, friend. But let me warn you now, no-one has ever found no treasure, nor the ship herself for that matter."

"The odds have been the same all my life," Rokura replied.

The fellow slapped him on the shoulder. "Spoken like a true gambler."

He smiled. "So, you seem to know about the ship. I bet you've spoken to a fair share of people like me."

"Plenty, at that."

"Then, any advice? I've spent a little time in the port, but I've never sailed the reefs. Don't even know much about the treasure, either – only that it's supposed to be a significant haul."

"You must know at least the story of her final voyage, then?"

"A few bits and pieces. Some say that it was a storm. Or

sabotage, depending on who you ask."

"Close enough – it was both," he said, leaning against the rail now. "You see, the captain was carrying sensitive cargo between Makmir and Senoja, and all went well until the final leg – navigating the reefs. Obviously, over the centuries, enough has been harvested or cut by the sorcerers so the passage isn't too difficult if your helmsman is paying attention, but the storm darkened everything that night."

"And, combined with sabotage..."

"Right. Most folks say it was due to cargo being *smuggled* aboard the *Shark* that she ran afoul of the reef, cargo the captain was not aware of."

"Weapons from the Senoja, I was told. To be used to repel Nasaru raiders."

"Yes. And so the story goes that Captain Noomu learned of this and smashed all the lights and smashed the helm while he was at it."

"Was he actually so patriotic to doom his ship, the lives of his men and his own life like that?"

"That's where plenty of folks like to argue," the first mate replied. He raised a finger. "But some gaffers tell a tale that differs again. This time, Captain Noomu *is* aware. He's a Takirov sympathiser and very much wants to bring the weapons to port, only his crew mutiny against him. Yet not all aboard the *Silver Shark* are loyal to the nation and in the struggle, the ship and everyone aboard is lost."

Rokura raised an eyebrow. "That I've not heard. But whatever the truth, I don't know if it will help me. I think I'll need charts, a ship and divers. Or some magic to locate the *Shark*, surely?"

"So you will. And you won't be the first to try as much but I've told you that story for a reason, friend."

"Oh?"

"Because even if you are the one to finally find her, or to break through whatever magic or luck has cloaked her from treasure-hunters for all these years, you have to think carefully about who to approach once we dock."

"Why is that? I don't imagine anyone will be thrilled to see yet another treasure-hunter, but are you telling me I'll be… what, jailed or driven out of Makmir for asking?"

"I'm sure there are some that would do as much, but not everyone knows that His Majesty will seize a mighty *four-fifths* of whatever you find. So, if you approach a Nasaru captain once you return to port, you'll have to give up nearly everything," he said with a shrug. "Now, more than many have been willing to try, so even a fifth of a fortune is probably worth it."

"And that's something all captains will declare?"

The first mate spread his hands. "On the surface. But then, the closer to a pirate a captain has become, the less chance his client will have of returning, right? No point finding the treasure if *you* end up replacing it at the bottom of the ocean."

"What if my captain were Takirov?"

"Haha, yes. That's the right question to ask, of course. But that's not much better, I'm afraid. If you find one willing, they're going to be more desperate than most, since they'll be risking death."

"Death? For searching for a wreck?"

"Aye. Thanks to the Takirov's role in the smuggling of the past, today, no ship flying Takirov colours is permitted to search for the *Silver Shark*."

Unwelcome complications, one after the other.

Yet using a Nasaru ship wouldn't be much better than risking a Takirov flag. After all, when it came to dividing the treasure, what captain would let a *nobody* pick and choose? More, any interest shown to the red box would mark it as too important to give away.

A Greyshield could have taken anything, suffering no objection.

Even a lord.

Maybe I ought to have asked the Mistress for help after all.

Rokura hid a clenched hand at his side. Would it be so bad to earn something without a lifetime of advantage? *I don't need the cloak to live the code. I can help Iggy and save Asaro, Fara, and the others without it.*

And the last time he checked, the disc still had Brutan and the prisoners due south. It was such an unerring path that it seemed they, too, were heading for the sea. Or perhaps their hideout lurked someplace within the significantly larger capital, home of the bulk of the Coral trade?

"Having second thoughts?" the first mate asked.

Rokura smiled. "By now, it would be a lot more than second thoughts."

"Well, I wish you luck," he said. "And Gods know I've said it before, but I do mean it, friend – you worked hard and offered no complaints, seems a shame to lose a good man."

CHAPTER 40. – ROKURA

Port city Makmir was smaller than the capital, but it stood larger in Rokura's mind as he stared across at its pastel colours – grey tree trunks and dark leaves with orange undersides in the gardens. Most were quite large too; the sort of trees said to reside in the eastern islands.

Domed rooves peered above the gardens, these in the same bluestone seen elsewhere in the south, and from nearby, splashing echoed from one of the rock pools. Even in such a simple inn with only two pools; one for cleaning objects, and the other for food. One of the attendants was probably adding treated Coral-powder to the water.

Rokura leant forward against the balcony rail, steel cool beneath his forearms – only to straighten slowly at what he saw in the street below.

A figure in a red cloak, accompanied by a Greyshield, heading for the docks.

Princess Kiteka.

She still wore her greying hair tied into a tail. She walked with one hand upon the hilt of her blade, but she was smiling, not glaring at her partner. Another familiar face.

Greyshield Edazol.

An imposing man, tall and slender, whose whip-like movements on the battlefield concealed a hidden strength, a weight of stroke that seemed beyond muscle and bone. Like few Rokura had faced before, both as a novice and as a man upon the sparring grounds.

Had they come to Makmir in connection with the duke after all? It hardly seemed likely, but their presence alone raised questions...

Rokura returned to the main room and its single bed, where Iggy still lay sleeping. The lad needed rest after spending so long out of sight in the dimness of their river journey – and stepping out for a short while ought not endanger him. Few things *could* trouble the young man in the end, considering his power.

And the mysterious Nuka would be watching.

"Rest well," he murmured as he closed and locked the balcony doors, drawing the shade after. Then, he crossed the room and paused at the exit. Leaving a note might have been a possibility with another travelling companion, but in the absence of such a choice, he would simply have to return swiftly.

In the hallway, Rokura passed a display of rainbow-coloured shells in various shapes, barely pausing in the busy common room before returning to the streets. There, he kept pace with a small crowd of dock workers in plain smocks, quickening his step further. The figures of Kiteka and Edazol receded as they neared the docks.

Rokura kept them within sight but did not close much distance, leaning against the warm walls of a bakery a moment. The scent of fresh bread was almost tempting enough to delay him, but he continued on. At the next cross-street, he had to push through locals and Nasaru alike, but on the other side, he slowed to pass beneath the sculpture of a mighty whale where it spanned the entry to the docks, as if admiring the workmanship.

And it was magnificent, especially the detail upon the tail, with barnacles of a paler stone.

But Her Highness and protector were his true objects of interest; they had stopped to speak to the captain of a three-masted ship, one conspicuously not flying royal colours. Why not take advantage of her station?

She is hiding something. I was not wrong.

Rokura crossed to the opposite side of the pier, feet stirring scales and dust alike, to where a boy was selling cheap fishing poles. He stopped to buy one, offering a smile as he did. While the lad chattered about where the best fishing spots could be found, Rokura nodded along but kept an ear on the not-too-distant conversation.

It seemed the princess was hiring the captain to take her to common smuggler's dens... searching for who or what, exactly?

"Rokura. The black does not suit you."

Rokura turned to find Edazol regarding him with a sad smile, half-hidden beneath the grey of his moustache. The kind expression did not quite reach his steely eyes, but the concern *was* present. It was only that the man's facade was so unaccustomed to faltering, and so it had been over a decade of training.

"Master," he replied, almost without thinking. "It is a pleasant surprise to see you here."

The man's smile grew warmer. "Surprise? Well, that cannot

be so – you marked us from your window, did you not?"

Rokura did not know whether to sigh, chuckle or frown. "Her Highness is far from Atanoph."

"That she is." Edazol did not elaborate, he merely waited.

It's like he still cannot help himself. But without bitterness, Rokura answered. "I cannot imagine she is here to pay captains to be on the lookout for me."

"Of course not," he replied. "That, you should be able to discern yourself. And in regard to the matter of your temporary departure from our ranks, I would dearly like to hear what you have to say on that matter." He raised a slender finger. "However, not until you explain your mysterious Senoja companion."

"I am helping the lad travel a strange land."

Edazol nodded. "You hesitate."

"I do."

His old mentor gestured to a winding set of stairs that led down to the water, where only a single fisherman waited at the farthest point of the pier. Rokura glanced to where Princess Kiteka spoke to another sailor, from the next ship.

"No bitterness, lad."

Rokura shook his head. "I appreciate being called 'lad'. I don't hear it so often now there's a little grey to my beard."

"Wait until you get to my age," the man replied as he started down the stair.

At the bottom, he leant on the rail but did not stare across the harbour with its green water and slow-bobbing hulls. "Something makes you hold back. Do not disappoint me and claim it is ill will."

Rokura shrugged. "Why not?"

"Then what of the Code?"

"I do not need it to do what is right," he replied, and while the words were delivered without faltering, it would be hard to convince Edazol. *Especially as my own doubts do not seem to vanish as I'd like.*

Edazol stroked his moustache. "And withholding information about your Senoja charge meets your new 'criteria'?"

"I will share one thing only. He does not hail from Senoja."

The man raised a grey eyebrow. "I see."

"Though I know I offer little, I would ask if you and the princess are here to seek Duke Bedoa and his... important charge." *Yet what other reason would exist – aside from treachery. And does that seem likely, despite my suspicions, my so-called 'proof'?*

"Are you offering your assistance, then?"

Rokura did not answer immediately. "Under certain conditions."

"I do not envision a lot of success should you seek to negotiate with Princess Kiteka."

"Then we can strive for a common goal without sharing the road," Rokura replied.

"That would be something I will let Her Highness decide, of course."

"Then Asaro was here?" Rokura kept his voice soft.

Edazol tilted his head, a slight movement only. "We have yet to confirm that. But our Sorcerer *has* confirmed your report at least; they have come south. And if it is a ship they seek, we will intervene, swift and horrible."

"Just the three of you?"

"Half a squad in town and more coming from the local

garrison, but if we are not careful we may miss our chance while waiting. We may already have missed it."

"Where are they hiding?" Rokura asked. "My disc says south of here, still. Probably the capital."

"We do not know for certain," Edazol replied. "If you want our guess, I will need to know more about your young friend."

"That is a confidence I will not betray."

"It is not a betrayal if it is in service to your nation, Former Lord Rokura." A new voice spoke from the steps.

Rokura turned. The princess was approaching, hilt of her blade visible when her cloak opened. Her expression was expectant, but he did not go to a knee, nor did he offer his own weapons, as was once customary.

Instead, he bowed his head. "On that I believe we disagree, Your Highness."

"Yet I would appreciate your considerable skills, now that you are here, vassal or no."

He met her gaze. "It is not my desire to inconvenience you. But despite our common goal, I believe I have a different path to walk."

"On that common goal you will follow my lead," she replied with a frown, then started back up the steps. "Edazol, bring him aboard."

Rokura turned back to his old mentor, who spread his hands. "As I said, the decision is hers."

CHAPTER 41. – ROKURA

The ship Princess Kiteka had hired afforded them use of the captain's room – spacious enough for desk, bed and wardrobe – though the man doubtless had been given little choice in the matter.

And while the woman's summary of her own search for Brutan explained something of the connection between him and Duke Bedoa, the finer details were lost on Rokura; the red velvet box from the Mistress' vision rested on the table. It was clean and dry, a golden lock in its centre.

A sense of power – threatening power – poured from within. Similar, but more impatient than what he recalled from Nuka...

"Former Lord Rokura, do you understand what I am expecting?"

"That I accompany your force to Viareya, where you believe Asaro is already being taken, even now." Somehow, still, the thought of travelling so far, to a new continent, of leaving and thus exposing Iggy to dangers of being alone, or questions of why the duke would be heading to the arid lands, all played second fiddle to the box.

Could it actually be what the Mistress of Obsidian sought? How?

The princess sighed. "I remember you as far more astute."

"You do?"

"That is not all I require. We will be bringing your charge with us."

"That is not a decision for me to make," Rokura replied, keeping his tone even enough – yet the words... the words were not something he could have uttered before being struck from the ranks of Greyshield.

Edazol straightened from where he leant against the windows, his shadow moving with him. "Rokura –"

Princess Kiteka raised a hand. "Rokura, understand that I am not asking you to convince the young man. I am telling you what will happen. The nation cannot bear a failure now and I know that you are aware the lives of dozens of children may still be saved. But only if we act swiftly."

Rokura met her gaze. His next words could not be rushed. "I would love to hear that the children can be saved."

She rose from the chair. "I had hoped to have your cooperation willingly."

"That chance was lost when you demanded I betray Iggy."

"Lad, this isn't a battle you can win," Edazol said, his voice firm. "Nor is it one you *need* to fight. You said yourself that we share a common goal."

Rokura gestured to the red velvet between them. "If that is in fact true, will you explain the box to me – it bears an ill feeling."

"A rather clumsy query," the princess said. "And one I believe you know the answer to, since it is why you are protecting that boy."

"Your Highness?"

"No more delays. You know this is a relic, the very one you seek at that – something quite powerful and not at all anything that ought to be placed into the wrong hands."

How had they found it? *Why* had they searched for it in the first place?

And how do they know that is what Iggy is seeking?

He did not reply.

"I am losing what little patience I have. Our sorcerers are aware of precisely why you are here, and let me tell you that this item will not be delivered into the hands of our enemies, no matter how well-meaning your intentions may be."

Had they interrogated, or stolen the information from Cosequ?

It no longer mattered.

Despite her claims, Kiteka was still incorrect about at least one thing – Iggy. For whatever reason, they still had not discovered – or perhaps did not believe – that he was from the village of Nokema, at least.

Perhaps they did not even know what the lad was capable of.

"I will help you hunt down Brutan," he replied. "But not with Iggy."

Blinding light flashed.

When the room cleared, Iggy stood near to the table, his dark hair free of the hood, his smooth face revealing nothing, yet to Rokura it was clear he was still somewhat weary by the way he stood, feet braced.

The princess had fallen from her chair, only now reaching her knees. Had Iggy attacked when he arrived?

Edazol's eyes had widened, apparently shocked but unharmed as he pointed with his blade. "Do not move, youngling."

Iggy stood poised between the man and the box, shoulders trembling now. With rage or fear? Fear seemed unlikely. Exhaustion?

Rokura. I can take either you or the box and escape, but not both.

Rokura glanced between the two – the Princess was still rising, rubbing at her eyes – and he nodded to Iggy. There was only one answer. "Take the box."

Rokura… are you certain?

Edazol hissed. "I said halt!"

"You are faster, Iggy," Rokura said softly.

Thank you, my friend.

Edazol swung his arm. A blade flashed across the cabin but Iggy was already a blazing streak of blinding white.

When Rokura's vision cleared, the captain's desk was empty and Iggy gone.

All that remained was a sword, one edge bloodied.

ACKNOWLEDGMENTS

To each and everyone who supported this trilogy on Kickstarter, thank you so much, these books are for you.

It's been a long wait - but without everyone below, the wait would have gone on and on and there would have been absolutely *zero chance* that all three books would have been released together, so thank you again!

Heiko Koenig ~ Vitor Publishing ~ Jeff Lewis ~ Daryl Parat ~ Jesper Pettersen ~ Larry Couch ~ Supreme Emperor Ben Mariner ~ The Creative Fund by BackerKit ~ Stephen Ballentine ~ Esapekka Eriksson ~ John Idlor ~ David Lars Chamberlain ~ Robin Hill ~ Virginia McClain ~ Señor Neo ~ John Mackie ~ Jason Cordero ~ Richard Bunting ~ Debbie Phillips ~ Jason ~ L.M. Lacee ~ William C. Tracy ~ Erin Himrod ~ C.Wilson ~ Sven Lugar ~ Ian Linford ~ Monica Elida Forssell ~ Astridd ~ Technewszone.com ~ Samantha Landstrom ~ Anne Walker ~ Cheryl Linford ~ Zac ~ Shirley S ~ Richard Novak ~ nny ~ Aramanth Dawe ~ Thomas Polk

~ Maddalena Tarallo ~ Donna ~ Mitchell S. ~ Trava Buono ~ Lee Dunning ~ Levid José de Jesús Montes Sánchez ~ Scott Freisthler ~ Peter & Andy ~ Fritha Blackwood ~ Leo Collis ~ Jamie-Lee Graafmans ~ Michaela Miles ~ Belinda Mellor ~ Katherine Shipman ~ Patty Jansen ~ Jessica Ward ~ Jazmine Baldwin ~ C. Gockel ~ Sven Grams ~ Matthian ~ Scott Freisthler ~ Rhianne R. ~ Blade ~ Emma Adams ~ C.Niehot ~ Becky James ~ sabrinaweb71 ~ Tony and Ben Muzi ~ Joe Monson ~ Tao Wong ~ Zee ~ Ellen Pilcher ~ Jesper Pettersen ~ Award-Winning Author Wendy Scott

I am also once again in debt to Brooke! And to Rebekah at Vivid Covers for the amazing set of covers that not only showcase the main cast, but strike the perfect mood.

I must also thank Amanda at Phoenix Editing for always going beyond what I ask (especially with Volume 3!) and also David at David Schembri Studios for the formatting – I know I gave him some extra work with the range of fonts!

Ashley Capes

A NOTE FROM ASHLEY

Hello! I hope you enjoyed *The Faceless Moon* and thank you for reading.

If you could help me out by leaving an honest review of the book at your place of purchase, that would be fantastic! Long or short, bad or good, it all helps.

As all three volumes of the Exiles Trilogy were released together, you can already sample or purchase *Exiles: Volume 3 (Stars Burning)* at your retailer of choice!

AND if you'd like to sign up to my newsletter (https://www.subscribepage.com/b5w1k0) you'll be the first to know when future Exiles books are released. You'll also have first access to preview chapters and pre-release editions of my other stories, in addition to being automatically added into the draw for giveaways.

Ashley

www.ingramcontent.com/pod-product-compliance
Lightning Source LLC
Chambersburg PA
CBHW020355120726
47904CB00002B/577